ALANA GRAY

Rough Cut Romance

First edition

ISBN: 978-1-0675358-0-3

This book was professionally typeset on Reedsy.
Find out more at reedsy.com

Contents

Free Book! iv
Rough Cut Romance v
Chapter One 1
Chapter Two 5
Chapter Three 10
Chapter Four 15
Chapter Five 19
Chapter Six 23
Chapter Seven 28
Chapter Eight 33
Chapter Nine 38
Chapter Ten 41
Chapter Eleven 46
Chapter Twelve 52
Chapter Thirteen 58
Chapter Fourteen 63
Chapter Fifteen 68
Chapter Sixteen 75
Chapter Seventeen 79
Chapter Eighteen 86
Epilogue - Six Months Later 90
Check out my full catalog! 95
About the Author 97

Free Book!

Scan the QR code to see a full book list and subscribe to my newsletter

Alana Gray

Rough Cut Romance

She built up her walls—he showed up with a chainsaw.

Vera

My divorce is finalized, my son is heading to college, and for the first time in years… my life is peaceful.

Almost.

Because college tuition is outrageously expensive, and peaceful doesn't exactly pay the bills.

So I do what any slightly desperate single mom with construction experience and a questionable sense of humor would do—I start designing nightstands.

Normal nightstands… with one tiny twist.

Each one has a hidden compartment for mommy's *special toys.*

Because no parent wants their kid discovering what's tucked into a drawer or hidden under a mattress and waving it around for the world to see.

The idea is brilliant.

The timing? Not so much.

The trade show that could make this business take off is only a few weeks away, and my design still needs serious work.

Enter Wyatt.

A ridiculously talented carpenter with a crooked grin, endless patience, and a goofy sense of humor that makes me laugh harder than I have in years.

Between sawdust-filled afternoons in the workshop and road trips for supplies, we fall into an easy rhythm.

The kind that feels dangerously close to something more.

Which is a problem, because I just fought my way back to peace.

And the last thing this newly divorced single mom needs is another man complicating her life.

Wyatt

I was raised by a single mom who worked herself to the bone while dating a parade of men who made her life harder.

I promised myself I'd never be one of those guys.

No drama. No messy relationships. And definitely no getting involved with a woman who already has enough on her plate.

Then Vera asks me to help build her "toy chest."

Next thing I know, I'm spending every spare hour helping her design nightstands with clever hidden compartments and sexy little secrets.

Working with her should be simple.

But Vera's smart, funny, and stronger than she realizes. And somewhere between sanding wood, testing sliding panels, and hearing the story behind her crazy idea…

I stop wanting to keep my distance.

She deserves someone steady. Someone who makes her life easier.

The problem is…

The more time we spend alone in that workshop, the harder it is not to imagine being the reason she doesn't need those toys anymore.

And if I'm not careful, this little side project might turn into the one thing I swore I'd never risk.

My heart.

Chapter One

Vera

I don't think ten inches will fit, let alone twelve.

I thunked my head against the table. The enormous dildo that had been lying in front of me rolled off and hit the ground with an impressive thunk.

I don't know why I thought this was a good idea. I needed to bring in more money if I wanted to help Benji with his tuition when he went off to college this fall.

Since my ex and I split five years ago, making ends meet has been more of a stretch. I thought a side hustle like selling these custom-made, multipurpose nightstands would be a perfect idea. Every parent could relate to the fear of their kid discovering their sex toys. A hidden compartment built into a sleek, attractively designed nightstand was the answer.

The problem was I had no idea how to design anything, or run a business, for that matter.

In a panic, I'd walked into Wild Timber Homes a week ago, a custom home builder in the area, and spilled my guts to the woman working in the office. She'd said she'd given my name and number to one of the carpenters, but the guy hadn't called yet.

It was fine. I could do this on my own. I was just hoping to get a little expertise so I could get this project off the ground in time to help my son. I knew how to build; I just needed someone who could help me with the innovation part.

There was a trade show coming up in two weeks. It always had lots of small home-based businesses, people selling soap and knitted or quilted items. I could get a ton of orders for these if I just had something to show at the event. Then once I'd built one, I could build a heap of them, different colors, different dimensions with the same hidden secret.

But it had to fit the biggest toys you could buy. If it couldn't take a whole foot of cock, then I could lose out on buyers. The design ideas I'd been playing with weren't cutting it.

It had to be big, but also look sleek. Kids were smart. If it were obvious, they would find it.

"What's for dinner?" My son walked past me, seemingly without noticing the dildo on the ground.

I guess not all kids were good at finding things.

I carefully kicked the toy under the table as Benji poked his nose into the fridge. He had just turned eighteen and was always hungry. Luckily, I could take home some leftovers from the diner where I worked. "There's soup and breadsticks, but I'll make something more later."

"Score," he glanced at me over his shoulder as he pulled containers from the fridge. He had his father's looks. Boy next door, blond hair and blue eyes. I was lucky he hadn't made me a grandma as young as I'd made my mom one, although there was still time. "You okay, Mom?" he asked.

I nodded. "Just trying to stretch a dollar."

He frowned. "You don't need to help me with college, I told you that already. I've got some money saved from my summer job at Two Rivers Tree Falling, and Brody promised me some weekend work was coming up soon."

I sighed. That wouldn't be enough. Even if he lived at home, it wouldn't be enough, and I knew he had his heart set on the dorms. Springwood Technical Institute was only a forty-five minute drive from here, but that would make for long days if he had to commute. "It's my job to worry, kiddo."

He slid a bowl of soup into the microwave and sat down across from me. "I'm not a kid, Mom."

No matter how old he got, he would always be my kid, but I knew he didn't want to hear that right now. And whether he expected me to help him or not, I still intended to. Assuming I could figure out how to get this goddamn design right.

My phone vibrated on the table.

Wild Timber Homes flashed on the screen.

I answered, quickly stepping away from the table so Benji wouldn't hear. I'd tell him my business plan eventually, but not until I had it up and running.

"Hello?"

"Hi, this is Wyatt calling from Wild Timber Homes. Our office manager, Layne, said you needed help with a small project?"

I breathed out a sigh. "Yes, I'm trying to build a prototype for a furniture design and I...I'm stuck," I admitted, failing to keep the desperation I was feeling from leeching into my voice.

Asking for help was a shit feeling.

"We can sort it out together," his voice was light and reassuring. "I'll need to see what you're working on. I can come to you."

I sank onto the couch. "That would be great." The simple sound of the man's voice calmed my rapid heart rate.

We made plans for him to stop by, a time when I knew Benji wouldn't be home, and I set the phone aside.

"Who was that?" Benji asked, appearing at the door with a bowl of soup in his hand. "Got a date?"

He seemed intent on getting me to date lately. Probably because he was leaving for school and didn't want me to be alone.

But I had just gotten back to a sense of peace after the turmoil of my divorce. The divorce had been amicable, Scott and I were still friends, but dividing up a life that had been intertwined for nineteen years wasn't easy.

I wasn't eager to disturb my new sense of calm for a silly dream about love. Besides, between working at the diner, getting this business going, and keeping track of Benji, I had no time for anything more.

Chapter Two

Wyatt

"I'm headed out, Bossman," I called to Jace as I grabbed my tools.

He raised an eyebrow.

"He's talking to a potential client about a side project," Layne said, elbowing Jace. "Remember?"

Jace's eyebrows rose, and he nodded quickly. "Right, forget about that. Uh, let us know how it goes."

"Okay," I said, confused by their reaction. I took on side projects all the time when we were slow. Why they were acting all weird about this one, I had no idea. I'm sure they would just miss me.

I got into my Wild Timber Homes truck and started the engine. Wildrose Bend was a tiny place, all things considered, so it wouldn't take me long to get there. Even if I hit the one stoplight in town on a red, it wasn't exactly rush hour.

I arrived at my destination in no time and I parked my big

white diesel in front of the house, then grabbed my tool belt and secured it around my waist. I was used to building homes so building furniture would be a piece of cake. Which was perfect.

Work was actually smoking busy, but we were waiting on materials for a big project we affectionately called the Beast. It was a hurry up and wait game, and I couldn't handle standing still.

I glanced up at the house as I walked up the driveway. It was a small place with a one car garage and a loose gutter to the left of the door. I made a mental note to mention it to the homeowner. Hell, I could fix it while I was here if they wanted me to. My brain automatically made a list of repairs wherever I went. My mom always said I'd try to fix heaven's front gate if they ever let me in.

I knocked on the door, and a moment later it swung open. I opened my mouth to introduce myself, but no words came out. The woman in front of me had her dirty blonde hair pulled back from her face. She was wearing light blue jeans and a t-shirt, arms with visible muscle on display. I was six feet tall, more with my boots on, and she wasn't far behind. Her blue eyes were big and round, and there was a small smile on her light pink lips.

So much for my professional greeting. My brain had apparently clocked out early.

"You must be Wyatt," she said, her smile widening. "I'm Vera."

She stuck out her hand. I gripped it in mine, and shook it. "You look familiar," I blurted.

Real smooth, Wyatt. Next, ask if she comes here often.

Her cheeks colored, and she let her hand fall from mine. "Oh, uh, I wait tables at The Bent Rose if you're ever there."

I nodded. "This town only has so many places to eat, and

Bent Rose is great, so I'm there all the time."

She moved past my awkwardness, and stepped back. "Come on in."

I stepped into her house; it was tidy and well kept smelling like something delicious. Meatloaf, maybe. I expected her to lead me to the garage, but we ended up at the kitchen table.

She sank into a chair, and I followed suit.

I glanced around the table. There was a notebook with the corners rolled from use, a ruler, a pencil, and a collection of items that made my cheeks burn red.

"Uh, are those...relevant to the project?"

She followed my gaze, looking completely unfazed. "Oh, yes," she flipped through her notebook, but didn't explain why she had what looked like dildos and vibrators in a variety of sizes in the middle of her kitchen.

"Ah, here we go," she said, turning the notebook in my direction. I studied the image. It was a carefully hand-drawn blueprint for a small dresser or nightstand. "Okay, that looks simple enough."

She let out a long, aggravated groan. "That's what I thought too, but there's a curveball."

I blinked. "Care to fill me in?"

"Do you have kids, Wyatt?" She rested her head in her hand.

I shook my head, trying to keep up with her train of thought. Pretty sure we'd taken a sharp turn somewhere after I noticed the sex toys, and I was lost.

She nodded. "Well, kids have a way of embarrassing their parents, either with what they say or what they do. I can tell you from experience that they can come across mommy's special toys and decide to parade them out into the living room when your in-laws are over, or mention them to strangers at the grocery store."

"By special toys you mean…" I gestured towards the sex toys, and she nodded. I fought to push down the image that was building in my mind of her using one of the vibrating bullets, sliding it between her thighs and making her own legs quake. The full HD mental picture my brain supplied was extremely unhelpful.

"Okay, I can see that being a problem, but what's this got to do with the furniture?"

Her eyes lit and she tapped the drawing. "I want to design a nightstand with built-in hidden storage for things you don't want your kids to stumble across. I know how to build a nightstand. I used to work in construction. What I can't figure out is the design. So, basically all I have is an idea, a nail gun, and enough sex toys to make a porn star blush."

I wondered if she bought the toys to test the nightstand design or if she already had them. Again, not a helpful thought. "So you need me to help with the initial design, and build for your, uh, toy box?"

She laughed. It was a pretty sound that made my chest feel light. "Toy box, oh man, that is a great name for this. Do you mind if I use it?"

"Go ahead."

"I'm not just building this for myself; I want to make a business out of it."

I blinked a few times, slotting all the information she'd given me into place. She mentioned a kid, and she mentioned in-laws, which implied there was a husband in the mix somewhere. Disappointment settled low in my gut, although when I glanced at her left hand there was no ring on her finger.

I should be focusing on the design, but her relationship status felt more important.

"So you're married," I blurted, my brain going from two steps behind to ten steps ahead.

She shook her head, "Divorced, single mom to one very strong-minded eighteen-year-old boy. I don't have to worry about this with him anymore, but I bet lots of parents do."

Single? Yes! Single mom? This new information tempered my excitement.

Not that I had anything against single moms; I was raised by one. That experience is exactly why I usually keep my distance. I watched my mom try over and over again to find love, only to find one more obligation. One more person to take care of. I did everything I could to help her out: took on odd jobs, cleaned the house, and told every stupid joke I could come up with to make her smile. I would never want to be one of those guys like my mom dated. Demanding attention from someone who was already overworked.

"Is that something you can do?" She asked, pulling me out of my own head. "I know Wild Timber is known for custom builds, but this is a bit different from a cabin or house."

A nightstand wasn't exactly the Taj Mahal, but adding an element like hidden storage could be tricky. I knew I was going to say yes to whatever she needed from me. I was invested in this strange little vision she had, and I wanted to help her.

My curiosity about her collection, and what she did with it had nothing to do with it. Okay, maybe a little to do with it.

"Leave it with me. I'll go over your design ideas and we'll come up with something." So long as I could keep myself from being distracted by my sexy new client. And the most awkward kitchen table meeting of my professional career.

Chapter Three

Vera

"Hey, Ruth," I said, grabbing an apron off the hook and tying it around my waist.

"Hey," she called over her shoulder, grabbing two big plates from the window and hustling them over to table four. She was the owner of the Bent Rose, but you'd never know it seeing her work. She wasn't one to hide out in the back office.

The lunch rush had clearly already started, and I grabbed a notepad and pencil to get going. I headed toward the first table, but slowed as I recognized the woman sitting there.

She was the manager of the Wild Timber Homes office.

Glancing at the other people at the table, my eyes landed on the back of one man's head. His hair was dark and a little on the longer side, not scruffy, more tousled in a way that made me think he ran his hands through it a lot. I couldn't say that running my hands through it hadn't crossed my mind when he'd shown up at my house the day before. But I'd been too desperate for help with my project to get distracted by the good-looking carpenter.

"Good morning, folks. Can I bring anyone a coffee to start?"

I was expecting Wyatt to pretend he didn't know who I was. After all, I was the weird single mom who'd burst into his life looking for help to build a box to hide vibrators. But that's not what happened.

"Vera! Hi. I've been working on trying to figure out your design problem. I don't think I got any sleep last night, actually. It's just such an interesting puzzle to try to solve. The combination of making sure the product looks good but also functions for hiding—"

The woman from the office elbowed his ribs, and he clamped his mouth shut.

"Maybe it's better to talk with her about this when she's not in the middle of a busy restaurant," she said.

Wyatt's ears turned red, and he nodded. "In that case, I'll have a black coffee, please."

There was a murmur of agreement around the table, and I scooted back behind the counter to grab the coffeepot. As I turned around to head back to their table, I bumped right into Wyatt.

I wasn't much shorter than he was, but still my forehead almost collided with his chin; the arm holding the coffee pot hitting his solid chest. He caught me by the shoulders before I could fall back, and the heat of his hands sank into my shoulder through my polyester uniform. "Sorry, I almost spilled hot coffee on you."

"No, no, it's my fault." His hands stayed on my shoulders, and I made no move to step away. "I just wanted to apologize for bringing up your project in front of a bunch of people while you're at work. I was just really excited about trying to solve your design problem."

I tilted my head. He really was cute. It was sweet that he'd thought to apologize, and that he was as excited about my project as I was. Maybe even more so.

I was trying to solve a problem, but my goal in solving it was mostly to help my son pay for tuition.

Wyatt's interest seemed to be partly professional curiosity and partly wanting to help me. It had been a long time since someone had wanted to help me just for the sake of being a nice person. With his too-long hair almost covering his eyes and his bright smile, he was unlike a lot of men I'd met while working blue-collar jobs.

Many people in the trades were hard. Maybe they'd had rough lives, or maybe they'd become hard from the long hours of physical work. But Wyatt didn't seem to fit the mold. He had a golden-retriever, happy-go-lucky attitude that was as refreshing as it was strange.

"No need to apologize. It's not like you said exactly what the hidden compartment was for. Besides, I'm really excited to have your help."

His smile grew wider, and he pulled his hands away and tucked them into his pockets. The move looked almost boyish, even though the man had to be in his late thirties, if not older. He gave a single nod. "In that case, I should let you get back to work. We can talk about design later." He turned and walked back to his table.

I filled their coffee cups and then set about my usual tasks, but before I could approach a second table, Benji came to the counter and took a seat.

I frowned. "What's wrong?"

He shook his head. "Nothing. I forgot my house key so I need yours. Who was that guy you were talking to?"

I fought the urge to roll my eyes. I knew Benji was interested in getting me to date, but surely he wouldn't try to push me together with every man in Wildrose Bend.

"That's Wyatt. He might be giving me a hand on a furniture restoration project I was thinking about."

He nodded. "I know who he is. I know who all the people at Wild Timber Homes are. I did a project on them for my engineering class last semester, remember?"

I hadn't actually remembered that, and guilt gnawed at my gut.

I tried to take an interest in all the things my son did.

He was a really smart kid.

I had always been better with my hands, taking things apart and putting them back together. But Benji had an academic understanding of math, engineering, and structures that I never had. Not even after working in construction on and off for most of my life.

That was what he planned to study when he went to Springwood Technical Institute. He hadn't decided what area of engineering yet, but I had a feeling his career path would overlap with what they did at Wild Timber Homes.

"Well, why don't you go over and say hello, then?"

He bit the side of his lip. "Is it weird if I just go over there and start gushing about all the homes they've built? I'd like to know more about what they do. What kind of software they use. Some things I didn't think to ask when I did my project before, but I'm starting to think about now that I'm picking my college classes."

I tucked the bit of awkwardness between Wyatt and me aside

and went into full mom mode. I flipped over the cup on the counter in front of Benji and filled it with coffee. Decaf, because I was still his mom.

I caught Wyatt's eye over the back of the bench seating and crooked my finger at him. His eyes went a little wide, and red crept up his neck, but he stood and walked over to the counter.

I put an arm over my son's shoulder, and he immediately tried to shrug me off. "Wyatt, this is my son, Benji."

"Mom, it's just Ben," he interrupted.

I pursed my lips. "Fine. Wyatt, this is my son, Ben. He's going to be going to Springwood Technical Institute after he graduates, and he's interested in engineering and architecture."

Wyatt stuck out his hand. "Good to meet you, Ben. I do some work with those subjects myself."

"I know, I'd love to ask you about it, if you don't mind." Ben was blushing, but he held Wyatt's eye and pride rushed through me.

Wyatt grabbed the seat next to him and sat down. I had one of those moments where I was struck by how grown-up my kid was, and had to step away.

Seeing Wyatt interact with him was something I needed to distance myself from, too. Wyatt was cute and kind, but I'd fought hard for the peace I had in life now, as chaotic as it was. I couldn't risk it even for a pair of pretty brown eyes.

Chapter Four

Wyatt

"I'm definitely not an engineer, but can tell you whatever you want to know about what we do at Wild Timber."

"That would be great," Ben took an awkward sip of his coffee. I made a mental note to call him Ben, not Benji, since that was what he preferred.

I remembered being his age. It had always been just my mom and me, and well before I was ready for the responsibility, I'd taken on any job I could get, trying to help with the bills that never stopped coming. I'd started off as a laborer, working my way up before taking some courses in CAD and basic design. That was how I eventually landed my job at Wild Timber Homes.

It would have helped if I'd had someone already in the industry back then, someone I trusted to give me advice. I might not have my own kids, but that didn't mean I couldn't offer a little wisdom to someone else's. If I could save the kid from at least one dumb mistake, he'd be ahead of where I was at eighteen.

"I do most of the computer work for the designs. I'm the only one with the patience for the software."

Ben perked up. "What kind of software do you use?"

I babbled on for a while about the programs we used and my workflow. As I told him about the Beast project we were working on, Vera appeared and set plates of food in front of both of us. I'd been so distracted I hadn't even ordered, but someone must have told her what I liked. The plate of pancakes, eggs, and sausage was exactly what I would have chosen.

"So, when are you off to college?"

Ben swallowed a mouthful of French toast. "September, but hoping to move to Springwood in June. I work a bit for Two Rivers Tree Falling, and they have more work in Springwood than here."

I nodded. "I've worked with the owner, Brody, on a few projects. He knows his stuff."

Ben nodded. "That's part of why I want to get more hours in with him. But I also need the money. School will be expensive."

"How expensive?"

He shrugged. "Crazy expensive. But I've had summer jobs since I was fifteen, so I've got some money saved up. I've applied for scholarships, and I plan to work while I'm in school. My mom keeps saying she's going to come up with a way to make extra money, but I don't want her to worry."

I absorbed that. As the kid of a single mom, I understood the dynamic between Ben and Vera better than most. If her nightstand idea was a way to help Ben, I was even more invested in making it work. That little *toy box* project felt a lot less like a weird side job and a lot more like something important.

"What about your dad?" I asked, spearing some scrambled eggs, and taking a bite.

Ben wiped his mouth with a napkin. "He's great; he and Mom get along fine, luckily. But he's a long-haul trucker, so he's away a lot, and that isn't exactly a high-paying job either. Mom and Dad both work really hard. I don't want either of them to think they have to help me with college. But I know both of them do."

He seemed to have more on his mind, so I waited him out.

"They had me when they were like twenty, so when I'm halfway through my degree, they'd have been buying diapers. I know they feel responsible for me, but if they could raise a kid at my age, surely I can figure out how to cover my own expenses, you know?"

I did know.

I saw a lot of myself in the kid. Even though his dad was in his life and mine hadn't been, I understood what it was like to feel responsible for your parents in some way.

"Tell you what," I said, setting my fork down. Somehow my plate was empty, and I didn't remember finishing it. "I'm no expert, but if you ever have questions or want to stop by Wild Timber Homes to see what we do, feel free. Helps to see how the industry works from the inside."

Ben's eyes lit up, then flicked over my shoulder. Before she even said a word, I knew Vera was standing behind me.

"Benji doesn't need more things to do. He needs to focus on his studies."

"Mom, my grades are fine," he said. "And if I can learn more now, it'll be easier to do well in my classes once I get to college."

There was a hint of defiance in his voice, but not an ounce of disrespect. I remember that age, feeling like a man, but being treated like a boy. Like you were one good decision away from opening the door to adulthood, but everyone kept hiding the keys.

Vera turned her gaze on me. "You really don't have to."

I nodded quickly. "I know, but I want to."

Vera looked from me to Ben, then over to the table where my boss and coworkers were still eating, and finally nodded.

"Okay. Thank you, this is something I just can't help him with."

A wide smile broke over Ben's face, and I could see how Vera still saw him as a kid; he looked like he'd just been invited to Disneyland. "Let me give you my number. Anything you need, just call or text. It doesn't hurt to have a friend in the industry that you're trying to get into."

As I typed my number into Ben's phone, I glanced up and saw Vera watching us with a smile on her face. For as much as she worried about her son, it was clear she would do what was best for him, even if it meant letting someone else in. Which, for reasons I didn't want to examine too closely, made me feel about ten feet tall.

Chapter Five

Vera

I had wanted to ask Wyatt more about his thoughts on the nightstand design, but every time I was near the front counter, he and Benji were in deep conversation.

Benji's dad, Scott, and I had led different lives than what Benji was pursuing. We had both gone into the trades. We struggled to help our son with his last year of high school and preparing for college. Benji and Wyatt seemed to bond over their interest in design and engineering, and I didn't want to interrupt them.

The rest of my shift flew by. I wasn't even sure when Benji and Wyatt took off. When I got home, I had a text from Wyatt.

Wyatt: I have a few ideas I wanted to run by you. Let me know when you're free.

Vera: I'm not working tomorrow

I didn't want to seem too eager, but I had to get this design done. I was also curious to talk to him about Benji. Wyatt seemed like a good guy, smart and sexy…

Wait, I didn't need to be thinking about him as sexy.

I had a hard time accepting help, and somehow I had accepted his help with my business idea and my son. I couldn't go another step, and bring sex into the mix.

Besides, why would a good-looking guy like him want to date a struggling single mom?

Wyatt: Can we meet at my place? I've got things set up in my garage so we can figure the design out.

I sent him a thumbs-up, and he texted back an address.

The next morning was Sunday, and Benji was still sleeping when I got up. After coffee, breakfast, and *not* agonizing over what to wear, I got in my SUV and drove to the address Wyatt sent me.

Wildrose Bend was a small town as it was, but his place was even more rural than the town itself.

His property was extensive, with a wire fence around it, and a meandering dirt driveway. It was thick with trees in places and bare in others. If I had never met Wyatt, I would say it had serial killer vibes, but given what I knew of him, it was a symptom of a busy mind.

There were a few vehicles on blocks and stacks of lumber off to one side. The house came into view, and it was clear a home builder owned the place.

It was stunning.

A log home like the kind he built, all peaked roof and smooth logs. An enormous wrap-around deck extended across the front, and elaborate rock work covered the beams.

There was a detached garage with three bay doors. It wasn't as fancy as the house, a basic tin structure, but one of the bay doors was open. I drove towards it and parked.

As I was getting out of the driver's seat, I turned to see Wyatt coming out of the garage.

Shirtless.

My heel caught on the lip of the footwell, and I grabbed the door to keep from falling.

Holy shit.

The man was a work of art.

It was only May, but the day was warm, and he had clearly been working hard. There was a sheen of sweat over the muscles of his chest. His lean pecs and abs were on full display, and I found myself wanting to trace every peak and valley with my tongue.

"Hey DIY Diva, you found me," he said with a smile.

I blinked out of my daze. "I did. Nice place."

He nodded his thanks. "Want to see what I've been working on?"

I nodded eagerly and followed him.

The radio played softly in the background as we stepped into the shop. The ground was hard-packed dirt, but still dust puffed under our feet as we walked inside. Benches and shelves lined the walls, with tools everywhere. I'm sure he understood the system, but to me it looked like someone had picked up the entire garage and shaken it.

A dresser with all its drawers pulled out sat in the middle of the floor.

"I pulled the dresser from my room and dragged it out here. I needed to see where we could add something that would work."

I smirked. "Wow, you are really dedicated to my project."

He shrugged, and it made the muscles of his shoulder dance under his skin. "I'm invested now; it will drive me crazy if we don't come up with a solution."

He scratched his head and sawdust fell onto his shoulder. I had to stop myself from reaching out to brush it from his skin.

I pushed the thought away. "My original thought was to either have a false bottom on a drawer or a false top on the stand itself that lifts up. But since the user would need to access the compartment often, neither of those is a great option."

He twisted his lips in thought. "Right, you'd have to either keep the top and drawer empty or move everything when you need something from the compartment."

"Exactly."

"What about something that slides out from the side?"

We passed ideas back and forth, looking for a solution. Examining the way the slides worked, flipping the drawers over to spark ideas. We actually worked well together. He was knowledgeable and creative, and I had done my research on what a potential client might want.

The clock was ticking until the trade show, and I had a list of things to do that was a mile long. I had to figure this out, build the prototype, refine the design, print order forms and business cards.

I had to stay focused.

The problem was our compatibility was hard to ignore, and so was my growing attraction.

Chapter Six

Wyatt

"Does this really not already exist?" I asked as we examined the dresser from all angles. Maybe if there were something similar we could look at, it would help us figure this out.

She signed. "Based on my research, there are versions of it, but mainly to hide valuable jewelry or to have a weapon close by. Jewelry is way smaller than what I want to hide, so it is not a good option. And since guns have to be in a safe in Canada, the ones meant for weapons aren't really sold here. I think I've found a niche if I can get the size I need."

If I were talking to one of the guys, I would have made a joke about 'having the size she needed'. Actually, if the guys were here, we'd already be on joke number twelve, and probably crying with laughter because, despite all being adults who did taxes, we were basically twelve-year-old boys when it came to humor.

What I felt for her didn't feel like a joke though, and heat spread through me.

The fact that this entire project came back to sex toys didn't help the situation. It was putting questions and images in my mind that I really didn't need floating around there.

Which of the toys that I'd seen on her table were her favorite?

What did she look like when she used them?

Did she hide in the dark like she was doing something naughty, or slide the toy between her thighs anytime the mood struck?

Once again, I pushed the thought away.

"So this is really a problem people have?" I asked as we continued to play around with ideas. She was close enough that I could smell her shampoo, something soft and warm, and feel the heat off her shoulder.

We'd already circled this topic, but I couldn't help wondering why this was a better solution than just keeping things in a closet or whatever.

"Yep, I asked around in some mom groups on social media to see if it was something people might buy before I started trying to design it."

I nodded, my eyebrows coming together.

She glanced at me. "I can see you still have questions."

"I just wonder why someone would keep things in a nightstand if they are worried their kid will find it."

She laughed. "You know in movies when the male character says he's going to rock her world all night long?"

Heat pooled in my groin at her words, and I nodded. "Well, when you have kids, the *all night long* part is getting up to change diapers and get them a drink of water or whatever. So your sex life is broken down into little snippets of time whenever you can get them. You need all the supplies close by."

"Need to be prepared for a quickie at any moment?" I asked, willing my dick to stay calm.

She moved, leaning over me to examine the drawer slide. "Bingo. Since bed is the most comfortable place to have sex, the nightstand it is. Get all cozy under the covers, turn to the person next to you, and go to town."

I swallowed. I knew she meant in bed, but it wasn't lost on me that as she said it, I was the one next to her. Plus, she was hypothetically talking about some very *not* hypothetical things that were getting me *not* hypothetically turned on.

"What about the shower? Seems like you'd have more privacy there." My breathing was shallower than it should have been, and my overactive imagination was constructing images in overdrive.

She bit her lip. "With kids, showers are tricky. You can't hear them cry over the sound of the water. Hell, when Benji was small it was a challenge just to get a shower at all."

"What if your kid was older, say, in high school?" She glanced over at me. "For example," I added quickly.

She licked her lips and held my eyes. "That's a different story. They do make waterproof toys so people can have fun in the shower. Alone or…not. I mean, you'd already be naked, hands sliding over your skin. Soap making things all slippery." Her eyes dropped to my mouth, and my lips parted in a gasp.

I'd been crushing on the single mom since I first saw her, eager to help her with her project. I'd resisted asking her out because I knew she had a full plate and I didn't want to be the one to have it overflow and fall apart. Besides, I hadn't picked up any vibe that she might be interested in me until right now, as we sat close enough to share air between us.

Should I take a chance and make a move, or pull away?

Before I could make up my mind, she blinked and looked away. "Maybe I can make a version of this that can work with a bathroom vanity, if we get the design sorted out."

The moment, whatever it had been, was gone. For her, anyway. My cock was half hard down the leg of my shorts and I hoped it deflated before she noticed.

She stood. "Well, I think having something that pulls open on the side, like how you open a box to mail a letter, would work the best. What do you think?"

I thought we should reenact what she said about hands sliding over skin, but I couldn't say that. "I agree, why don't we try to build a basic one, and go from there?"

She nodded, and we got to work.

A nightstand isn't a complicated design, and we both had experience building things, so we had a prototype put together from scrap wood I had lying around in no time.

Vera grabbed the tape measure and took a few measurements of the pull-out on the side. "It's big enough to fit the biggest toys," she confirmed. "Couldn't fit a ton of them in there at once, but I think it will do the job."

She beamed at me and I basked in its glow. I was such a sucker.

"So where do we go from here?" I asked, wiping a bead of sweat from my forehead with the back of my hand.

"I need to get some nice quality wood, cherry or oak maybe? I'll see what they have at the hardware store in Springwood. I'll get a few different stains too, then build a working model I can display."

"I can help," I said.

Her brows furrowed. "You've already done so much—"

"I don't mind; I love a good trip to the hardware store."

Her face softened, and she smiled. "Alright then. Road trip. Your truck or my SUV?"

Chapter Seven

Vera

We took Wyatt's truck.

Probably for the best. I had taken my SUV on lumber runs before, but it hadn't been pretty, and I didn't want to risk the expensive wood getting dented. I settled into the passenger seat, watching as Wyatt rested one hand on the top of the steering wheel. His skin was a patchwork of cuts and old scars, not so different from my own when I used to work construction. Skilled or not, we all got bumps, bruises, scrapes, and splinters.

We sat in companionable silence as we made the forty-five-minute drive to Springwood. The silence was nice, not awkward—just there. We made it to the hardware store, and Wyatt carefully backed his truck into a parking stall. It was a warm day, and I turned my face up to enjoy the sun.

Once we were in the store, he grabbed a wheely cart, and started moving through the aisles.

Chapter Seven

We spent a full hour looking at different wood, hinges, stains, and drawer pulls. I grabbed brushes and screws, too. By the time we were done, I was getting tired. "Hungry? I owe you dinner for all the help," I asked as we carefully slid the planks into the bed of his truck.

"Can't say no to that. I'm starving. What do you feel like?"

"Anything but diner food. I get enough of that at work."

He laughed. "Understandable. Okay, how about sushi?"

We found a place nearby and grabbed a table by the window. Music played low in the background, and I could smell seaweed and something savory.

Once we had placed our order, we relaxed into the vinyl booth, checking our phones and taking in the buzz of the busy restaurant around us.

I wanted to get to know him better, even though, if this design worked, we really wouldn't need to see each other much anymore.

The server arrived with our appetizers. A series of items each on its own plate. She put them between us, and we dug in.

He broke the ice before I thought of a topic. "I had fun talking to Ben the other day. He's a great kid."

"Thanks," I said, tracing the rim of my teacup with a finger. Steam curled up, smelling faintly of jasmine. "I think so, too. Too smart for his own good. He's got a mind for numbers."

"I wish I could relate on the math front," Wyatt said, leaning back in the vinyl booth. Sunlight slanted across the table, glinting off his watch. "There's a reason I never became an architect or an engineer. But we have a lot in common, anyway. I was raised by a single mom, too."

I sipped the green tea the server had left at our table. "What's your mom like?"

His face softened. "The hardest-working person I know. My dad left before I was born, and she kept everything going."

"That must have been rough on both of you."

"It was," he explained, his normally smiling face was somber. "She lost her sense of humor along the way, so I made it my job to bring it back. I would always try to make her laugh. Then, once I was old enough, I helped with chores and bills, and things got a bit easier."

"So you've always been a hard-working guy."

He nodded. "Mom made me what I am today."

"And what is that?" I asked, tilting my head, trying to lighten up our serious conversation.

"Handy, handsome, and hilarious."

I laughed, leaning a little closer. "Well, you're not wrong."

His cheeks went a little pink. "What has being a single parent made you?"

I huffed a breath while I thought about it. The first thing that came to mind was *tired*, but that felt too heavy. There were moments when that was how it felt, but it was balanced with other things. Other moments when I knew that all the hard parts were worth it. "I guess it made me stubborn and determined."

"You must have been those things already if you worked construction. That job is not for the faint of heart."

I laughed, thinking about the early mornings, the cold, the heat, the heavy work boots. "Some guys were pretty rough around the edges, but once I proved myself, it was a lot of work, but a lot of fun."

"I worked it too, back before joining Wild Timber. Man, for a teenager, I learned a lot of things I probably shouldn't have from the guys I worked with."

I laughed. "Oh, I can only imagine. I remember it well."

"My favorite insult they threw around was, 'You must have been a C-section baby, the way you avoid labor.'"

I snorted. "I never heard that one. I always loved, 'I do more by accident than you do on purpose.'"

He laughed and put his hands on his hips. "'Go apologize to the tree for the oxygen you wasted.'"

"Or, 'I've had footballs sharper than you.'" I added.

"Razing was definitely part of the job. I remember this new guy started once. Cocky as all hell. At the end of his first day, the foreman told him, 'You're about as useful as the share button on a porn site.' His ego deflated after that," Wyatt said, eyes sparkling.

"Rookies always got it the worst. 'What are you, neither-handed?'"

"'If I wanted someone to watch me work, I'd have become a stripper.'" I covered my mouth, trying not to snort.

"Or the safety advice. 'Don't stick your hand where you wouldn't stick your dick.'"

The word *dick* from his lips made me clench my thighs together, but even so, we were cracking up.

The server approached, eyeing us as she placed a selection of sushi rolls on the table. The sesame smell made my mouth water.

Wyatt pointed at one of the rolls with his chopsticks. "That one is thick enough to need a special nightstand compartment."

I choked on the bite of sashimi. "Warn a girl before you say things like that; I almost died."

"Sorry, just saying."

"Great, now I can't eat a dynamite roll without thinking about dick."

His eyes darkened and held mine for a heated moment. He slid the plate with the large roll across the table. "You better have it then."

The heat between my thighs got more intense. "You want that on my mind?" I asked, spinning my chopsticks between my fingers, a teasing smile on my face.

"Depends who's dick you're thinking about."

I felt my cheeks heat and could see Wyatt's doing the same. We didn't break eye contact—not when I picked up a piece of the roll with my chopsticks, not when I slid it into my mouth. Something that sounded like a low groan slipped between his lips. The idea of throwing some cash down on the table, pulling him into the parking lot, and sliding into the back seat of his truck came to mind.

"How is everything so far?" the server asked, her voice breaking the spell between us. I hadn't even seen her approach.

"Uh, yes, great. Thank you."

"Wonderful," Wyatt added, clearing his throat.

She collected a few used plates, smiled politely, and walked away. The moment was broken—which was for the best. How many times did I have to remind myself that I didn't want to complicate my hard-won peace? A few dick jokes shouldn't be enough to throw my desire for stability out the window.

I took a long drink of tea, letting the warmth settle in my chest, and we moved on to safer topics.

Although the more time I spent with Wyatt, the more I realized that no topic was completely safe.

Chapter Eight

Wyatt

It was dusk when I pulled into Vera's driveway. We both jumped down and started unloading the supplies, working together as if we'd been doing it for years. There wasn't much, but I was dawdling, eager to spend just a few more minutes with her.

It was rare to find someone who enjoyed my stupid sense of humor enough to give as good as they get.

We stood in front of her open garage door, light pouring out into the driveway. "Well, thanks for today," she said, shoving her hands into her back pockets.

"Yeah, I had fun," I said, looking down at my scuffed boots.

"I did too."

"You sound like the fun was unexpected," I teased.

She laughed. "I was just stressed about getting this design done."

"You're a good mom," I told her. "Doing all this to help Ben with his tuition."

She cocked her eyebrow. "How did you know that was why I was doing this?"

"I put two and two together from my conversation with him. You raised a good kid."

She shrugged. "I try. Doesn't leave much time for other things, though."

"Other things, like what?" I asked, shuffling a little closer, eager to rekindle the conversation we'd started at the restaurant.

She chewed her lower lip for a second, something that seemed out of character.

"Like spending time with a handsome man?" I asked. I was teasing. Sort of, I was also really curious about how she would answer.

She smiled. "You could say I've been deprived of handsome men."

She shuffled closer this time.

"Thank goodness I came along then. Otherwise, you'd have to supersize that toy box design."

"You haven't replaced them yet. They can do more than look good." Her eyes swept over me as she spoke.

"So you think I look good?"

"I do." Her eyes raked over me in a way I could almost feel.

My breath caught. The banter had taken a turn, and it was one I was very interested in continuing. "I can do more than look good. You don't even have to charge my battery." She smiled at my lame joke.

We were inches away now, sharing the same air. Her hands were still in her back pockets, pushing her breasts out until they almost touched my chest. I briefly forgot every word in the English language.

"Oh yeah? What's your first move?"

"A kiss is a nice place to start, a piece of rubber can't do that."

She smiled, her eyes dropping to my lips. "You're right," her voice was lower now. More intimate.

I brought my hand up to cup her jaw, running my thumb along her lower lip. Her skin was warm and soft under my palm. I moved forward to claim her lips, but just before contact, the door between the house and the garage flew open. "Mom, do we have any more of those energy drinks?"

Well. That was some Olympic-level bad timing.

She scratched her eyebrow and took a step away from me. My hand fell to my side. My dick gave an unhappy twitch. "Hello to you too, and you shouldn't drink those; you're eighteen."

"But—oh, hey Wyatt," his eyebrows dropped. "What are you guys doing together?" He walked a few paces closer and folded his arms across his chest. It reminded me of being caught with a girl by her dad when I was in high school.

Vera gestured to the pile of supplies. "I'm going to build custom nightstands, and sell them."

He glanced towards the stuff, then back at his mom. I felt like I shouldn't be here for this, but wasn't sure how to gracefully back away.

"For fun, or because you think I can't pay my own tuition?" Ben's face was solemn.

"Both. I have faith in you, kiddo, but life's expensive."

"I'm not a kid, Mom, I—"

They both seemed to remember I was there at the same time, and Vera turned back to face me. "I should head out," I said awkwardly.

She nodded. "Thanks again for today."

"No problem." And it wasn't, even if the evening didn't end

the way I wanted it to. A parent's work was never done; this interruption reminded me of why I had told myself to keep my distance. She didn't need one more person vying for her attention.

I got back behind the wheel of the truck, vibrating from how much fun I'd had with Vera and the fact that I knew if I had kissed her she would have kissed me back.

And I was absolutely going to think about that the entire drive home.

Probably longer.

******

The next day was Monday, and I had an entire week ahead of me working on the Beast. The client, Marin, had made change after change, and I was the only one with the patience to update the software. Which was less a compliment the more times I had to redo the plan.

The Wild Timber yard was a massive piece of property with lumber and machinery everywhere, not to mention workshops. I started my morning in the portable building that served as our main office.

"Morning, trouble," Layne called from behind her computer as I stepped through the door.

"I resent that nickname," I called back as I hung up my stuff.

"Then stop calling me *boss lady*."

"Never!" I called over my shoulder.

"How is your project going by the way?" I glanced in her direction. She had a cat that caught the canary look on her face, and I narrowed my eyes.

"You knew the details of what she wanted when you gave me

her number, didn't you?"

She cackled. "I may have."

"Well, jokes on you, she thinks I'm a delight, and it was not at all awkward when I walked into her house to see a pile of dildos on her kitchen table."

Layne doubled over laughing. I couldn't be mad, not when her joke had led me to meeting Vera.

"Alright, alright, it was a good one. I'll give you that."

Layne gave a little bow and got back to work.

Zane walked into the office a moment later, lunch kit in one hand and a file of papers in the other. "Morning, I talked to Marin about the Beast last night. She has more changes, but they are just tweaks."

I sighed. I had been mocking him about his communications with Marin, hinting that he had a crush, but after what happened yesterday, the jokes didn't feel as funny. Hard to tease a guy about flirting when I'd face-planted into my own almost-kiss situation.

"Alright, I'll get them added to the design."

Zane raised an eyebrow at my lack of a smart-ass response, but didn't comment.

I booted up the software and got to work. We were still dealing with material delays, but there were some things we could do and this was going to be a busy week.

I just had to keep my mind off Vera and get things done.

Chapter Nine

Vera

One day. That was all it took me to build the nightstand using the rough design Wyatt and I had come up with. The stain was still a little tacky, so I hadn't played around too much with the hidden side pocket design, but I was reasonably sure it would work.

The piece sat in the middle of my small workspace, proof that maybe this crazy idea of mine could turn into something real.

The trade show was on Saturday; today is Monday. I had a lot to do.

I used some of the wood scraps to make sample pieces of the stains I had to offer, and ran around town getting business cards and order forms printed. I practiced the things I would say to potential customers and toyed with the idea of a social media presence.

I was plagued by questions. What if I didn't sell any and this was a waste of time and money?

What if I overlooked some design issue and people demanded their money back?

I was literally picturing a horde of horny women storming my house with pitchforks and vibrators as weapons.

I needed to get out of the house. Luckily, I had a shift at the diner on Wednesday so I could focus on soup or salad instead of catastrophizing. I arrived earlier than necessary for my shift and slid behind the counter to grab an apron. "Hey, early bird, you miss me?" Ruth asked with a smile. She was around the same age as I was, but half a foot shorter, and her hair was dark where mine was light.

"Just needed a change of scenery," I said, tying the apron around my waist.

"Why not call up that handsome carpenter you were talking to last week?" She wiggled her eyebrows.

I sighed. The one good thing about worrying about my business was that I didn't have the brain cells left to think about Wyatt. We'd had so much fun together that day we'd gone to Springwood. We'd synced while we were working but also laughed until my stomach ached. And the almost kiss...

I pushed the thought away. It was a good thing Benji had interrupted. "I do enjoy that scenery," I admitted, "but he is exactly the distraction I don't need."

She gave me a look. "So you're just going to be celibate until life stops being complicated? Might be waiting a while."

I shot her a look. "This from a woman who is single, and works a hundred hours a week."

She planted her hands on her hips. "That's different."

"Oh, yeah, why?" I arched a brow.

"Because I don't have a sexy carpenter looking at me like he wants to eat me for lunch."

Blood rushed to my cheeks, and I straightened the napkin dispenser on the counter. "He does not look at me like that."

"So you're trying to tell me that everything between you is totally platonic? Never thought about kissing the man or taking him to bed?"

I pressed my lips together. And avoided her eyes.

"Thought so," she grabbed two full plates from the window and headed towards table seven. She bumped my hip with hers as she walked by. "You worry too much, hun. Think of dating less like risking your peace and more like sampling the buffet. You don't have to commit to the whole meal. Just try a bite, and if it's terrible, spit it out and go home."

"You know how long it's been since I sampled the buffet?" I muttered.

She laughed. "Might be time to get back to it then."

The diner was supposed to be a distraction but every time I had a second to spare, my mind wandered back to what Ruth had said. She was as hopelessly single as I was, so should I really take advice from her that she wasn't willing to take herself?

Then again, she was right, we were in different places in life despite being the same age. I was about to have an empty nest and I had a man who was not only interested but who I was compatible with.

Then again I had been compatible with Scott when we'd gotten together. That had ended in a divorce and a few rounds of therapy. I wasn't as young as I was when Scott and I had met either. I was older, maybe wiser although that was debatable, my priorities were different. I was looking for a good lay. Who wasn't? But that wasn't all I needed.

I had to feel secure in my own life, and taking a chance made me feel like the floor under me could tip at any moment.

Chapter Ten

Wyatt

Friday afternoon finally rolled around, and I went home from work to get cleaned up.

My boss, Jace, had invited all the people from Wild Timber Homes to his place for dinner. He did it every Friday.

It was a fun way to unwind at the end of the week. We also tended to have laborers come and go from the shop, so we got to know them at these things.

None of that was what was running through my mind, though. What I kept thinking about was Vera. I hadn't heard from her all week. I knew she was working on her project, so I shouldn't read too much into it. But the connection I'd felt between us last weekend was deeper than I'd felt before, and for that to just be gone was jarring.

I didn't like it.

Hanging out with my coworkers should provide the distraction I needed, so I didn't drive to her house and knock on her door and kiss her when I knew she was preparing for the trade show tomorrow.

"The party has arrived," I said as I walked through Jace's front door without knocking. Zane groaned from where he was standing in the kitchen with a beer in his hand. "You love me, don't deny it," I said, putting the case of beer I'd brought into the fridge.

I cracked one open, then spotted Layne smirking at me from across the room. "Did you have something you needed to say, boss lady?"

"Just wondering if you wanted to tell everyone about your project? A nightstand should be an easy project, right?"

She looked pleased with herself, I couldn't blame her for setting me up. I had been teasing her and Elias pretty mercilessly since they got together.

I sighed and sank into the couch next to her. "For a mere mortal it would be tricky, but she wanted a nightstand that would fit a giant cock and I am uniquely qualified to handle that challenge. It is a blessing and a curse being this well-endowed."

She punched me on the shoulder. "You did not just say that."

"Wait, why does the nightstand have a dick?" Sloane asked. Sloane was Layne's best friend and was currently dating her brother, Jace, who was everyone's boss at Wild Timber Homes.

Not a mess at all.

"No, the nightstand has a place to hide your dick; it doesn't have a dick itself."

"Oh because that would be too weird," Sloane said, throwing her hands up. "Who is putting their dick in a nightstand, and why?"

Jace and Elias walked in from where they had been barbecuing outside just as she said this and Elias raised a brow. "Do I want to know?"

Layne shook her head. "Probably not."

"Layne gave me a side job for a customer who wanted help to build a nightstand. Turns out she wanted a compartment hidden in it to hide her sex toys. Apparently, there is a market for it."

Sloane nodded. "I could see it."

Jace raised a brow. "You don't need toys, you have me," he said as he leaned over and kissed her.

"Well, you tell me where the vibrate button is on it, and I'll agree with you."

"Shots fired," I said with a laugh. "Anyway, the project is going well. The client, Vera, she's really cool to hang out with."

Zane appeared beside me, "You hung out with her?"

I shrugged and took a pull from my beer. "We had to drive to Springwood to get some supplies, went out for lunch; it was a lot of fun."

Elias and Layne exchanged a look. They had started dating four or five months ago, and had been attached at the hip ever since. "Does Wyatt have a crush?" she asked, making a baby voice.

"I am a grown man; I don't have crushes. I either want someone, or I don't."

"And do you?" Elias prompted.

I sank into a chair. "Dammit, yes, I do. But she's busy. She has a kid going off to college and is trying to make money with this nightstand project. I'm not sure she needs one more thing in her life."

"She's building sex toy storage, man, surely you can think of something you could add to her life," Jace said as he started setting food out on the table.

"I'm more than just a sex object," I deadpanned. Even though the idea of sex with Vera had me more than a little excited.

Layne stood up and crossed the room. "Look, Sloane and Jace didn't get together until twenty years after they started crushing on each other because they assumed I would be upset if my brother dated my best friend. Elias held off asking me out because he thought I had too much going on trying to get rid of my ex."

"What's your point?"

She flicked me in the center of my forehead.

"Ow."

"My point is don't assume you know what's good for her. She is a grown woman and has a teenage kid. She can decide what is and isn't right for her. Just talk to her for crying out loud."

"Communication? That's your advice? Have you met me? All I do is talk."

"No, you joke, and don't get me wrong, we all love laughing at you — er, with you — but it has to be deeper than that if it's the real deal."

I thought about this. "Well, we talked about our jobs in construction, her ex, her kid, her worries for the future. We talked about how I was raised by a single mom, and she is a single mom."

Layne clasped her hands in front of her chest. "Wyatt, did you have an adult conversation?"

I thought back over lunch with Vera. "I mean, we laughed a lot, but—"

"Oh my god, Wyatt's in love," Zane said.

"Am not." I crossed my arms over my chest, deflecting what he'd said.

"Alright, you hooligans, grab a plate," Jace said. "You can

torture Wyatt while we eat."

"Gee, thanks, Bossman," I mumbled.

"Always happy to help," he said with a wink before putting a baked potato on his plate.

The conversation mercifully moved off me eventually, not that I didn't deserve the razzing; I gave way more than I took. But what they said stuck with me. They were right. I was the jokester, but Vera and I had touched on topics I usually kept to myself. There was something more to what I was feeling for this girl, and maybe I needed to man up and tell her that.

Chapter Eleven

Vera

W*yatt: How is the assembly coming?*

I smiled at my phone like a weirdo and sent him a picture.

Wyatt: It looks fantastic. I'm working at the Wild Timber Homes booth at the trade show. I'll come by your table and check it out.

Vera: See you then!

My stomach did a strange little flip when I set my phone down. It had been a long time since a man texting me made me smile like that. And me replying with an exclamation point? Ugh, I had it bad.

The week flew by. And every spare moment after work was spent sanding, planning, pricing, or second-guessing myself.

Chapter Eleven

The morning of the show was a sunny Saturday. Two Rivers Tree Falling was doing a job in Wildrose Bend, so the owner, Brody, had picked up Benji before six for a shift. I had everything organized; all I had to do was load up the SUV and drive to the community center to set up.

The low murmur of voices met me as I stepped through the doors at the community center. Tables were set up everywhere, and people rushed from one to the next with boxes and banners.

"Are you a vendor?" a woman to my left asked as I stood there taking it all in.

I gave her my information, and she directed me to my table. A printed piece of paper that said *Toy Box* was taped to the middle of it, and I couldn't help but smile.

Seeing the name printed out like that made it feel real, not just an idea scribbled in a notebook between shifts at the diner.

I might actually pull this off.

I was arranging and rearranging the business cards, trying to keep my nerves from spiraling, when I heard heavy footsteps approaching.

"Wow, the finished product looks amazing."

Wyatt leaned forward to examine the nightstand. He looked unfairly good, his shaggy dark hair falling into his eyes, his wide shoulders stretching his trademark flannel.

My heart gave an annoying little skip at the sight of him.

"Wouldn't have come together without your help."

He shrugged. "You would've figured it out. All I did was drag my furniture around."

I laughed, and we locked eyes.

"I appreciate your help just the same."

For a moment, neither of us looked away. The noise of the room faded into the background, leaving just the two of us standing across the table.

He licked his lips. "I wanted to ask you—"

My phone rang noisily, cutting him off.

I gave Wyatt a sheepish look before pulling it from the back pocket of my jeans.

Benji flashed across the screen.

"Sorry, it's my kiddo. I have to get this."

He nodded, more understanding than a lot of people were who didn't have kids, and stepped back.

"Hey, hun. What's up?"

"Mom, I need some advice." His voice was tight.

My eyebrows dropped, and I glanced at my watch.

"Aren't you at work right now?"

Benji was quiet for a moment. "Yeah, we just..."

"What's wrong?"

Wyatt's posture changed instantly. The easy humor drained from his expression as he stepped closer.

"The guys felled the tree and then we were all going to take a break before we cleaned up. Brody and Levi went into town to grab us something to eat. I thought I'd start the cleanup, you know, impress the boss, but the homeowner is pushing me to drop another small tree for him, but—"

"But nothing. Your job is to clean up. You don't fall the trees, or run the dangerous equipment."

"That's what I told the guy, but he says it'll 'only take five minutes' and he'll complain to my boss if I don't get it done," Benji exhaled shakily.

I pursed my lips, trying to keep my temper intact. "You told him no, and he is still insisting?"

"I told him I'm not authorized. He said he's not paying if I don't do it." His voice lowered. "He's standing here watching me."

Wyatt, who had been leaning in listening, held out his hand silently. I put the phone on speaker.

"So Brody's not there?" Wyatt asked.

"No."

"Did you call him?"

"I don't want him to think I can't handle this."

"Don't do anything you aren't allowed to do," Wyatt said firmly.

"I know, I just... I don't want to lose this job."

Benji sounded so unsure. I hated this. I knew he took that job to help pay for college, but that was my responsibility—mine, and his dad's. It wasn't worth his potentially getting hurt.

I looked at my carefully laid-out table. The stack of order forms. I'd printed a ton of them, hoping this whole thing would work out.

Months of planning sat neatly arranged in front of me, waiting for customers who hadn't even walked through the door yet.

"The homeowner is trying to bully you into doing more work for him while the boss isn't there to see it. Brody would never discipline you for saying no to unsafe work," Wyatt said.

Wyatt was right, but my mom-brain needed action. Someone threatening my kid? Hell no. "Call Brody," I said. "In the meantime, text me the address. I'll come down there. I don't want you doing anything unsafe. Do you understand?"

"Yeah," his voice sounded resigned.

In the background, a muffled male voice barked, "You done gossiping yet?"

Wyatt's jaw ticked.

The easygoing man who had been joking with me seconds

earlier was gone. In his place stood someone much harder.

"Perfect," I said tightly. "I'll talk to you soon."

The call ended, and the noise of the trade show rushed back in around me.

I grabbed the box I'd brought my paperwork in and started stacking the order forms inside. My hands were shaking, and I wasn't sure if it was rage or disappointment, or something else.

Before I could get far, Wyatt caught my wrist gently.

"I have to go," I said. "I can't have him dealing with some angry homeowner alone. I'll stay with him until Brody gets back. I'll still get in a good amount of the event."

Wyatt shook his head.

I gestured helplessly. "I can't be in two places at once."

His expression softened. "You don't have to be. Give me the address."

"You're working."

"My guys can handle the booth for an hour. And even if they couldn't?" He shrugged. "It's lumber and brochures. Your son is doing a dangerous job with some bully breathing down his neck."

"I can handle my own responsibilities. You don't have to fix this."

"I'm not fixing it." His eyes held mine. "I'm backing him up. No eighteen-year-old should have to stare down a grown man alone, and you need to be here."

Something inside me shifted.

"I grew up watching my mom juggle everything by herself," he continued. "I know that look on your face. The one where you're already calculating how fast you can pack up and drive across town." He gave me a small, knowing smile. "Let me be an extra pair of hands."

I hesitated.

"And just so we're clear, I know you could handle this. I just don't want you to miss your chance to sell your spicy nightstands."

Despite everything, a breath of laughter escaped me.

"What if the guy gets aggressive?"

Wyatt's mouth twitched. "Then he'll get aggressive with a grown man, not an eighteen-year-old kid. Let me handle this."

My phone buzzed with Benji's text.

"I'll forward you the address."

He nodded. "I'll call you when this is sorted."

"Wyatt."

He paused.

"Thank you."

His gaze softened in a way that made my pulse stutter.

"You don't have to do everything alone."

Chapter Twelve

Wyatt

The address led me to a newer subdivision on the edge of town. An area where trees had been felled, and houses had been built shoulder to shoulder along the mountainside.

I parked to the right of the driveway and killed the engine.

Five minutes ago I'd been standing at Vera's booth trying to ask her out. Now I was the emergency backup for a teenage tree crew. I could see why she was tired.

Ben stood in the driveway, helmet off, gloves shoved into his back pocket. The look of relief on his face when he saw me was immediate.

A tall man in a polo shirt stood on the deck in front of the house, glaring down at me as I approached.

"You didn't have to come," Ben muttered when I reached him.

"Sure I did," I said lightly. "I was bored looking at brochures at the trade show. Another ten minutes, and I was going to buy a hot tub I didn't need."

The homeowner came marching down to the driveway. "If you're with the company, tell him to finish the job. I'm not paying for another visit because he's incompetent."

Ben squared his shoulders. "I'm not incompetent. I'm just not authorized."

Good kid.

I glanced toward the tree in question, studying it. The ground sloped toward the garage. The roots were lifting slightly on the far side.

I was no expert, but that wasn't a five-minute job. That was a *bring coffee, ropes, and three grown men* kind of job.

I stopped and looked at the homeowner. "Sir, this can't be safely taken down by one person. It's weighted toward your garage, and there are power lines overhead. The crew is coming back soon. They can do it right once they're here."

"It's barely bigger than a telephone pole," he scoffed. "He's got a chainsaw. What's the issue?"

My hunch had been right. If the guy didn't want to wait for the crew to get back, he probably wanted more work done than what he'd paid for. Probably thought he could intimidate the rookie into doing what he said.

Ben was made of tougher stuff than that. Must take after his mom.

"The issue," I said calmly, "is that if it kicks back wrong, it takes your garage roof with it. Or the fence. Or the power lines. And then your five-minute shortcut becomes a very expensive insurance claim." I gave the tree another look. "And I don't know about you, but I've never met an insurer eager to pay someone for a bad decision."

"You're making this more complicated than it needs to be."

"Yeah? Let me simplify it." I tipped my head toward the garage. "Nice roof. Be a shame if a tree fell on it."

The man crossed his arms. "I've dropped trees before, smart-ass."

"I don't doubt that," I replied. "But this is the type of thing that needs to be done right. And right means a full crew with proper tools and rigging."

"I already paid for tree removal," the homeowner said. "I expect the tree to be removed."

"And it will be," I said. "By the full crew."

The man and I stared at each other, me standing shoulder to shoulder with Ben. The homeowner's face reddened as Ben fought hard to look older than eighteen.

There was no way in hell Ben was touching that tree. I'd take him out of here myself if the homeowner didn't knock it off. Brody shouldn't be long though, Wildrose Bend wasn't a big place.

Just as I thought that, the rumble of an engine sounded, and I turned to see Brody's old truck pull in behind my Wild Timber Homes one.

Brody approached at a fast pace, eyebrows drawn low over his eyes. Levi wasn't far behind. We all knew each other just from being in the same industry.

"Ben, don't touch that tree. Wyatt, what are you doing on my job site?" Brody barked.

"Let's talk over here," I said, gesturing to my truck. "Before your customer decides I'm the tree-cutting police."

"Come on, rookie. Let's get these branches cleaned up," Levi said, guiding Ben away from the homeowner, and back to where they'd dropped the tree.

"Wait a second, what about my tree?" the homeowner said,

his voice calmer now that he was facing three grown men rather than a teenager.

Brody held up a hand, a gesture that invited no argument. "Let me handle this."

He and I walked over behind my truck to talk out of earshot.

Brody planted his feet, hands on his hips. He was a big guy, always in flannel like I was. A long, dark braid hung down his back, a nod to his Indigenous heritage.

"The homeowner was trying to push Ben to drop that tree by the garage, and he didn't know how to handle it."

Brody craned his head around to look at the tree I was gesturing to, and his lips pursed.

"I know, he called me while I was driving back."

"Guy was being an asshole."

Brody cursed. "Glad the kid didn't do it. That's not an easy drop."

I nodded. "I know. The kid didn't want you thinking he couldn't handle things, but he also knew he shouldn't do a dangerous job. Which, frankly, puts him ahead of about half the grown men I've worked with."

"I'll talk to him about it. I don't want someone on my crew to think they can't talk to me." He glanced back toward Ben, watching him for a moment with a thoughtful look that didn't match the usual grumpy-bear vibe. "Kid's solid. Just green."

I nodded.

"How did you end up here?"

I looked down at my work boots, kicking at the dry dirt. "He called his mom for advice and...I was with her."

Brody's face gave nothing away and he watched me carefully.

"We've gotten to know each other recently."

He remained silent.

"Fine. I kind of have a thing for her. Was going to ask her out before Ben called."

I leaned against the side of my truck. "Nothing like a potential chainsaw incident to really set the mood for romance. I'm a little out of my depth, though… I haven't wanted someone to say yes this much in a long time. Should I buy her flowers or something? I don't know."

Brody patted me on the shoulder. "I'm over forty and single, same as you. I'm the last person to take advice from. Every woman I've dated has said I'm a grumpy asshole and moved on." He scratched the back of his neck, an unexpected sign of vulnerability I'd never seen on him. "Hopefully, you have better luck than I did."

"You're not dead yet, man. Lots of time for romance."

He snorted. "Do I look like the wine and roses type?"

I thought of Vera—waiting tables, sanding and staining, and working construction. "No, but not all women want that. Some women prefer a guy who shows up when things get hard."

"Then ask her out," he said. "Worst thing she can say is no."

Little did he know how much that *no* would hurt if she said it.

He sighed. "Anyway, I better go deal with my customer."

I nodded and went to find Ben before I left.

When I found him, he and Levi were busily throwing branches into a chipper. I caught his eye and motioned him over.

"You okay?"

He nodded. "You really didn't have to come."

"I know. I would have worried if I hadn't."

He played with the hem of his shirt. "Mom would have worried, you mean?"

"We both would have."

"Are you and my mom, like… dating?"

I felt my cheeks heat, which was ridiculous. "No. Just friends."

"You want to be though."

Leave it to kids to hit the nail on the head. "That's between your mom and me."

"I'll take that as a yes." He smiled for the first time since I'd shown up. "That's why you showed up here right?"

I blew out a breath. "I showed up because I didn't want you to get hurt…if it happens to impress your mom, well that is a happy coincidence."

He laughed and shoved my shoulder. "I better get back to work. Thanks, Wyatt."

"Anytime." I watched him go, knowing things were fine with Brody and Levi here.

Ben may think I only showed up for Vera, but I had shown up for him too. I liked the kid and I didn't hate the idea of being one of the adults in his life that showed up for him.

Chapter Thirteen

Vera

For an event in a town this small, it was packed. I was thrilled, but the swirling in my stomach over what was going on with Benji hadn't settled.

Which was ridiculous. If I were this worried about a workplace issue, how would I handle him going to college?

Then again, he had called me. He was a smart kid, so if he was that worried, then there must be more than what he told me.

I reminded myself that Wyatt was there. Wyatt with his smart-ass mouth, and his helpful nature. Wyatt, who asked to help rather than having to be asked. Who understood why I hesitated when he offered.

I did my best to engage with potential customers. They were very complimentary of the design and the look of it. There were lots of laughs when I explained what it was designed for.

An hour into the event, I got my first order.

I shook the woman's hand, then put the order form in the box, staring down at it for a weirdly long time.

I might actually pull this off.

I took a deep breath, and when I glanced up, Wyatt was walking towards me with his usual casual gait.

My eye caught his across the space, and a slow smile spread across his lips. My stomach gave a little flutter. The look on his face told me that my son was fine, but it was more than that.

I was happy to see him in a way that went beyond my worries for Benji, and that was a feeling I hadn't had — in a romantic sense anyway — in a long ass time.

"Hey Nightstand Whisperer, how are sales going?"

I laughed at the silly nickname. "Tell me about Benji first."

"I'm glad he called, but Brody got there not long after me. He did the right thing by refusing unsafe work."

He was diminishing his own role in things, I was sure of it. His eyes were glued to my face with his smile still in place, and I tucked my hair behind my ear, feeling flushed under his stare. "Good, thank you. Really."

He shrugged. "So, tell me, sales?"

I reached down and grabbed my one sales form, and held it up. "I got my first sale."

That grin widened. "Congrats, that's amazing."

I tucked my precious form away. "It's a good start."

"An excellent start! We should celebrate." He licked his lips. "Can I take you out? To dinner, I mean, tomorrow night? I heard there's a new Italian place in Springwood that is fantastic. We can buy the wood for all the sales you're going to get today at the same time."

My cheeks heated. "Are you asking because you want to go to the hardware store, or is this a date?"

He leaned against the table. His scarred, rough hand contrasting with the smooth plastic top. "Two things can be true at once, but if we skipped the store and just went to dinner, I'd be okay with that."

I couldn't keep the smile off my face. "I have a morning shift at the diner tomorrow, but I'm free in the afternoon." I realized I was fiddling with my fingers and dropped my arms to my side.

"Good, great, okay. I'll text you. Good luck with the rest of the trade show. I should get back to my table."

I watched him go, worrying about tomorrow while being excited for it at the same time.

I ended the day with seventeen orders.

SEVENTEEN.

I all but floated out of the community center. Actually, floating would have been nice since my feet were aching. I had a lot of work to do to deliver the orders I'd taken, but I was feeling optimistic about my plan.

Not only that, but I had a date with Wyatt tomorrow night.

Benji texted that Brody had dropped him off, so I went straight home. "Hey, how did the day go?" I asked him as I put my things on the counter.

He was sitting at the table with a pile of grilled cheese sandwiches in front of him. "I'm sure you want the whole story."

I shook my head. "Only if you want to tell me. From what Wyatt said, you handled everything exactly right. I'm proud of you, kiddo."

"I'm not a kid, Mom."

I rolled my eyes. "Sorry, I'm proud of you, *young man*."

"Better," he took a big bite of his sandwich. "Are you going to date Wyatt?"

I paused and considered how I wanted to answer. This wasn't the first time Benji had asked. Maybe he saw what was growing between us. No parent wanted to talk about their dating life with their kid, but he wasn't exactly a baby. If something was going to happen between Wyatt and I, I'd have to talk to Benji about it eventually. "If I did, would you be okay with that?"

He nodded. "I don't want you to be alone when I go to college."

"Is that the only reason?"

He shrugged. "He seems like a good guy, and we get along. I think he's a good fit for you since he's so laid-back."

"Oh, and I'm not? Is that it?" I teased.

It was his turn to roll his eyes now. "You know what I mean."

"Yeah. I do, kid. Thanks for the stamp of approval."

I had given Benji a few more details about the business I was starting after Wyatt had left the other night. He had been less weirded out than I'd expected. Things were falling into place, and I was cautiously optimistic that I could help Benji and maybe be happy too.

******

I arrived at the diner the next morning before the breakfast rush. I could have used a few more hours of sleep, but I hadn't thought to ask for a different shift.

I yawned widely as I tied my apron around my waist. "Morning," Ruth said. "Get yourself a coffee before it gets busy here."

"I'll take you up on that."

I poured myself a cup and drank it black.

"How'd your trade show go yesterday?"

"Great, actually. It almost got derailed when Benji called needing some help, but Wyatt went instead so I could stay."

"Ooh, Wyatt, huh? Spending a lot of time with him these days."

"Well, I did hire him to help me with my project...and he asked me to dinner tonight."

I felt like jumping around in circles like a teenager and gushing about how cute he is. I held back...barely.

"That's exciting. You guys will have a blast. Are you excited? Nervous?"

I leaned against the counter. "I was nervous before. My life is a bit chaotic, but it works. If I am going to potentially throw myself off balance, it has to be worth it, you know? When he offered to help Benji, it was as if the concerns were lifted. He wasn't going to come into my life and take, take, take. He wanted to make my life easier. The fact that he and Benji have the same interests doesn't hurt either."

She squeezed my shoulder. "Happy for you, honey, just make sure you are picking him for you, not Benji."

My mom-brain would never let me *not* consider my son, but I wasn't only going out with Wyatt for that reason. There were a million reasons. He was hot, for one. But he was also helpful and kind. We had a lot in common, and dammit, the man was worth risking a broken heart for.

Chapter Fourteen

Wyatt

I stood in front of my closet, trying to decide what to wear. I'd narrowed it down to jeans and a t-shirt, or a t-shirt and jeans. That was literally all I owned. That our date was combined with a trip to buy construction supplies means that casual was the name of the game.

I was running out of time, and I didn't want to be late to pick up Vera so I grabbed my cleanest option, got dressed and headed out.

I pull up in front of her place to find Ben coming out the front door. He cracked a smile when he saw me. "So your plan to impress my mom worked, I see."

I blushed, which was ridiculous. "Laugh it up, funny guy."

"I will. Seriously though, do I have to give you the talk?"

"What talk is that? The birds and the bees?"

"Eww no," he shook his head. "No, no, no. I meant the whole 'if you hurt her, they'll never find your body'. That talk."

I laughed, and held my hands up. "That makes more sense. And I wouldn't dream of it. You can trust me."

"I do actually, which is why I'm not giving you this talk with a chainsaw in my hand."

"You forget I work with chainsaws too?"

He crossed his arms. "Just act intimidated so I can go to my friend's place, and you can get on with your date."

I pretended to cower, "I'll treat her like a queen, I promise."

"I prefer a goddess, but we can work up to that," Vera said, walking out the front door and turning to lock it behind her.

She was also wearing jeans and a t-shirt, and I mentally congratulated myself on nailing the date night look.

"Are you ready for our date, Goddess Vera?" I asked, bowing low.

She laughed, and Ben rolled his eyes. "I'll see you later Benji, be home by ten, okay?"

She ruffled his hair, then kissed his temple, and he pulled away. "Mom, that is so embarrassing."

"Fine, fine, goodbye."

She climbed into the truck and we were off.

"Did my kid give you a hard time?"

"It's his job as the man of the house, so I respect his commitment to his role. And as he will tell you, he's not a kid anymore."

She sighed. "I know, it's just hard to see Benji as anything but the little kid who was terrified of the bathtub until he was four and would only eat toast peanut-butter side down."

"He would hate that you told me that."

"At least I didn't break out the baby pictures."

I glanced at her in my periphery. "This isn't my place to say, and feel free to tell me to butt out, but you should call him Ben, instead of Benji."

I half expected her to fight me on it, but she sighed again, and ran a hand through her hair. "I know I should. I mean, that is literally what we named him, but he has been my little baby Benji since he learned to talk. I think letting go of it feels bigger than it is."

We were quiet for a moment, and I focused on the drive, worrying I had ruined our date before we had really started it.

"Do you think we can fit all the supplies for seventeen nightstands in the truck?"

I whipped my head around to look at her. "Seventeen? Is that how many you sold?"

She nodded. "I forgot I didn't tell you, yeah, that was how many paid orders I got at the trade show."

I patted her knee. "Vera, that's fantastic! Hell yeah, we can fit all that in the truck." We talked about what she would need to fulfill the orders as I drove, and before I knew it, I was pulling into the familiar parking lot outside the hardware store.

Since this was our second round shopping for this project, we got what we needed in record time, but by the time we had it all loaded in the truck; we were both sweaty and layered with dirt and wood shavings.

I looked down at myself. "I don't think I'm in any condition to go to a fancy Italian restaurant."

She laughed and dusted off her jeans. "Me either, should we pick somewhere more casual?"

I looked her over, this woman who'd had my head in knots for the last two weeks. Her hair was falling out of a loose ponytail; her shirt and jeans were dusty and probably smelled like lumber. Her hands had scars and cuts, just like mine did.

I'd come within inches of kissing her on more than one occasion. We'd joked about sex, danced around the subject over and over. Now we were finally on a date...although not a fancy one...and I didn't want to share her with the world for another second.

I stepped closer, moving slowly enough that she could tell me to buzz off if we weren't on the same page. I brought my hands to her hips and pulled her until we were pressed together. She brought her hands up and rested them lightly on my elbows.

"What's on your mind, Wyatt?" She teased with a smile.

"What if instead of taking you out, I take you to my place?"

"And what would we do there?"

I swayed my head back and forth as if I were thinking about it. "Get cleaned up. I could cook you dinner, and then maybe we could finally kiss without being interrupted by other people."

She hummed her agreement. "I think I might need an appetizer if I have to wait 'til we get back to your place for the main course." She ran her hands up over my biceps, then rested them on the tops of my shoulders, her eyes locked on my lips.

"I like the way you think."

Finally, I was able to close the distance between us — she might have actually met me halfway — and I tasted her for the first time. On the surface, it was all sweetness and minty lip balm, but underneath — where it counted — it was raw and desperate. Her arms tightened around me and I did the same, my hips pressed against hers, my rapidly hardening cock trapped between our bodies. Her breath caught as she moved her lips over mine. I gently bit her bottom lip before sweeping my tongue into her mouth. She held the hair at the base of my neck, guiding my head where she wanted it with the subtle sting of her grip. I wasn't much of a pain for pleasure guy, but this was working for me.

My fingers itched to roam over her body, and I was forgetting to breathe.

A car horn blared, and we pulled apart. Her cheeks were bright red, and I was sure I looked the same. "We need to get back to your place," she said.

"Get in the truck."

Chapter Fifteen

Vera

Wyatt pulled the truck onto the highway, and he stared intently at the road. He was a man on a mission, and I was absolutely here for it. "I really want to rub my hands over you right now, but I don't want to distract you while you're driving."

He huffed a laugh. "Telling me that is distracting me while I'm driving."

"Oh really? You should be thinking about what you're going to do when we get back to your place. There was a lot of big talk about how you were better than my toys."

He glanced over at me, and I held my breath. "Can't be that hard to beat them, toys don't have tongues."

I laughed. "One of them actually does."

He raised an eyebrow. "Seriously?"

I shrugged.

"What about one that has a tongue and can thrust inside you

at the same time?"

"Sorry, they have those too."

He breathed hard through his nose. "Alright, but can it do that and tease your nipples at the same time?"

"I mean, two toys could..."

He groaned and pretended to hit his forehead on the steering wheel. "You're going to give me performance anxiety."

I was teasing him and it was fun, but I was as turned on as he was and I knew without a doubt he would be better than anything I bought at the store.

Wyatt pulled up to a red light, and I unbuckled my seat belt, moved to the middle seat, and buckled up again. "Toy technology has come a long way, but it can't do this," I said, leaning over, and kissing a line down the side of his throat.

He groaned again, but for a different reason.

"Toys aren't warm and wet." I licked the skin I'd just kissed, and he shuddered.

"Besides, toys can't take their big body, and press me into the mattress, grinding against me until I lose my mind." I slid my hand over his cock through his jeans just once, then turned back to face the windshield.

"Fuck, you are so much better at dirty talk than I am."

The light turned green and Wyatt slammed his foot on the gas.

I laughed. "You can try again when we get to your place."

What followed was the longest drive of my life. I was pressed against his side, his heat leaching into me, his scent around me, and I was so turned on that the seam of my jeans was close to getting me off every time I shifted in my seat.

Finally, we pulled up in front of his house. He had barely shut off the truck before we were out and running for the house.

I crashed into his back when he stopped to unlock the door. Once it was open we both fell through it.

Wyatt slammed the door, grabbed my shoulders and pressed my back against it. He crowded against me, his hands on either side of my head, his hips against mine. "You were enjoying teasing me while I was driving, weren't you?"

I bit my lip and nodded. I knew funny Wyatt would enjoy the teasing, but this version of him, the sexy, determined, slightly feral one, would get payback in the best possible way.

"You knew I was going to want revenge even as you slid your tongue over my skin?"

I nodded again, running my fingers over his chest.

He moved back. "Uh uh, no touching for you." He took both my wrists in one of his hands and pressed them above my head.

My breath caught and my heart rate ticked up as he leaned in. All I could smell was his skin. All I could feel was the heat pouring off him.

My lips tingled at the thought that he was going to kiss me, but he bypassed my mouth and pressed his lips to the side of my neck.

I let my head loll to the side to give him better access.

The scrape of his stubble against the sensitive, neglected skin of my throat was positively sinful. He moved lower down, nipping and sucking as he went.

He reached my right nipple, still covered by two layers of fabric, and pulled it gently with his teeth. I gasped and let my head fall back as heat flooded my body.

"Take me to bed, Wyatt," I said, squirming under his mouth.

"Sure you wouldn't rather take your toy to bed," he asked. He got down on his knees, pushing the hem of my top out of the way with his free hand and kissing along the band of my jeans.

"Positive, I need you."

He groaned, dropping his head forward, his forehead resting on my stomach, his hair falling into his face. "I can't say no to that."

He shot to his feet and grabbed my hand before pulling me after him up the stairs, and into his room.

I didn't take the time to look around; I just moved towards the bed. He wrapped his arms around me, kissing me hard and fast. My back hit the mattress, and he landed on top of me, his hips notched between my thighs.

"What was it you said in the truck? Something about me pressing you into the mattress?" He asked as he rolled his hips against mine, grinding his length against my sensitive center.

I gasped. "I also said the toys weren't warm and wet."

He chuckled. "You're demanding."

"You like it."

"Can't argue there." He pushed off me and slid my shirt up my chest, kissing my stomach as he exposed more and more of my skin. I had the odd stretch mark from when I was pregnant with Benji. I may have been a young mom, but the kid was over nine pounds, and my body didn't bounce back like the magazines all said it should. The light pink stripes on my skin didn't even make Wyatt pause; he just kept going, kissing lower until he got to the top band of my jeans.

He popped the button, lowered the zipper, and I lifted my hips so he could strip me from the waist down. Once I was bare, he dove between my thighs like he was starving, roughly shoving my knees towards my chest and licking a stripe over my center.

I gripped the quilt, my mouth falling open as he teased me with light licks, and gentle nibbles.

I pushed my hips up, trying to encourage more friction. He evaded me, giving just enough to make me want more, but not enough to get close to the finish line.

When I growled in frustration, he pulled back and ran his tongue over his lower lip.

"Did you have something you wanted to say?" he teased.

I huffed. "Yes. You are far superior to my toys. You could put them out of business. The only way they can save themselves is to design one based on your tongue. Happy?"

He twisted his mouth like he was considering it.

"Oh, you tease." I grabbed his shoulders and pushed him onto his back, climbing over him to straddle his hips.

"Someone's eager," he said with a laugh.

I reached between us and palmed his cock, rubbing over the hard, thick outline. He grunted and cursed under his breath. I lowered the zipper and slipped my hand inside, feeling him through the thin cotton of his boxers. "Yes, someone *is* eager."

"Teasing is just mean when you do it," he said, eyes squeezed shut.

I laughed. "Let's just get naked then."

His eyes flew open. "I like the way you think."

We fumbled, pulling each other's shirts off. Wyatt shucked his jeans and boxers. We ended up naked except for socks, neither of us willing to wait another second.

We wound up in the same position again, him on his back with me straddling his hips.

I gripped his length, feeling the smooth hardness in my palm, and stroked him slowly.

"So much better than any toy," I said.

"Damn right," he replied, his voice strained.

"Mind if I take it for a proper test drive?"

"Can't say no to a lady."

I laughed, pushing up on my knees and guiding him to my entrance. I lowered myself down without taking my time. I needed him now, deep and hard, stretching me in the best way.

When I settled fully against him, we both gasped. I gripped his chest as I lifted and lowered again, a jolt of pleasure racing through me each time he filled me completely. I picked up the pace, adjusting the angle, chasing the high his body gave me. Sweat broke across my forehead as the heat of him soaked into me.

I was reduced to pure sensation, just feeling and needing more.

Suddenly he grabbed my hips, lifted me off him, and flipped me onto my back. I bounced against the mattress before I fully registered it.

He caught my legs and wrapped them around his hips, then drove back inside me. He moved like a man possessed.

I gripped his shoulders and bit gently at his neck, tasting the salt on his skin.

His pelvis pressed against my clit as he moved. I could smell his sweat and his soap, feel every inch of him as he drove into me, and then I was coming. My toes curled. I bit harder as my body seized and pleasure flooded through me.

"Fuck," he muttered as my muscles clenched around him. A second later, he followed.

I looked up at him, his dark hair falling into his face, his neck and chest tight with strain. God, he was so hot like this. I was seeing a side of him not many people ever would.

He collapsed over me, his chest rising fast against mine, still buried deep.

I fought to catch my breath. When he shifted, I felt his release slide out of me and realized he was bare.

"We didn't use anything," I said. "Last time I forgot, I ended up with Benji." I winced. "I'm on the pill now, though. Learned my lesson."

"I'm clean," Wyatt said, still breathing hard. "I promise."

"Same."

"Sorry. I forgot."

I caught his eyes. "I'm not. It felt amazing."

He rolled off me but stayed close, turning me onto my side and pulling me back against his chest. He kissed the back of my neck, then buried his face there with a quiet sigh.

I couldn't remember the last time I'd been this blissfully happy. Lying there, sweaty and spent in his arms, I realized how wrong my worries had been.

This was worth risking my peace for.

Chapter Sixteen

Wyatt

Thirty-two hours.

That was how long it had been since I dropped Vera off after our date.

That was how long it had been since I'd heard from her.

Did she think she had to wait two days before texting to not seem too eager or something?

I had been thinking about nothing but her, and it had been radio silence on her end.

I knew she was a busy person, but our date, as unconventional as it had been, was the best first date I'd ever had.

Once we'd finished in bed, we'd had a quick shower together, touching and kissing and exploring each other's bodies, before I'd made us dinner as I'd promised. Pasta because our plan had been an Italian restaurant. Jarred sauce because I didn't have a full day to make anything fancy. We'd sat on the couch eating pasta from bowls, me in my boxers, her looking sexy as fuck in my t-shirt.

We'd watched some DIY home renovation show and talked more about our days in construction.

I'd dropped her off after midnight. She didn't want to spend the night because of Ben.

Fair enough, made total sense to me at the time.

But why hadn't I heard from her since?

I was busy at work on Monday and enjoyed the distraction, but by the time I got home, I was desperate to know what the hell was going on.

I gave in and decided to text her. I typed into my phone.

Wyatt: Been thinking of you.

I backspaced and tried again; that was too needy.

Wyatt: WYD

No, I'm not a horny frat guy.

Wyatt: Still waiting on a status report. Did you throw out the toys after our date?

There, that was perfect. It was playful, fun and hinting at the fact that the sex was amazing. I hit send.

It was a full twenty-four hours, twenty-five and a half actually, before she texted me back, and by then I had run through every scenario in my head about what was going on. Rationally, I knew she was probably busy, but lying in bed, smelling her on my sheets, I imagined her hurt or injured, or I don't know, joining a cult and moving into the mountains.

Chapter Sixteen

Vera: Haven't had time

That was it. That was all she said.

Wyatt: Working at the diner?

Another half-hour went by.

Vera: Building the nightstands, lots of orders

Made sense; she was busy.

Her answers were short and invited no further conversation. Either she'd been taken over by an alien form, something I had considered in the dark, or the more logical conclusion that she didn't feel the way I did.

Or maybe I was right all along, and she didn't need one more thing in her life. After seeing my mom date, I swore I'd never be that guy who made a woman's life harder. Who was an obligation, not a partner. Somewhere between Saturday night and Monday morning, things had changed, and it wasn't for the better.

The workdays went by quickly in a blur of activity, but the evenings and nights were torture.

On Thursday, we ran into another delay of materials, and I was stuck twiddling my thumbs. I was sitting on the couch in the office, staring at the wall when Layne and Elias came in, holding hands and staring at each other with goo-goo eyes.

"Hey Wyatt, are you bored?"

"You have no idea."

"Why don't you go and see your girlfriend?" Layne asked. I had told her and anyone who would listen about how awesome our date was, minus the spicy details. That was before she started ghosting me.

"Things didn't work out, or aren't working out, I guess."

Layne frowned and came to sit next to me. "What happened?"

I dropped my head back on the couch, staring at the ceiling as I explained how the week had been going. The short texts or no reply at all.

"Have you called her? She's an adult. I think if she didn't want to do this with you, she would just say so."

"I don't want to be that guy, you know?"

"What guy? The one with adult communication skills?"

I shook my head. "She is making it clear she doesn't have time for one more thing in her life, and I don't want to make her life harder."

Layne shrugged. "Then don't."

"That's what I'm doing."

"Okay, true, you are not making her life harder, but you are also not making it any easier or better, right? I know what you said about your mom and not wanting to be a burden like some of those guys were. Well, show her you aren't a burden. Show her that you two can work together and make each other's lives better."

"How do I do that?"

"Depends on what the problem is, and to find that out, you're going to have to call her."

"Ugh, why is your answer to my problems always adult communication?" I teased Layne, but I knew she was right. I didn't want what we had to slip away, so I had to at least try to fight for it.

Chapter Seventeen

Vera

What comes after cloud nine?

Cloud ten?

Or is it just a deep feeling that you are totally screwed?

When Wyatt dropped me off after our date, I was on cloud nine. I was sore in the best places, satisfied in a way I hadn't been in a very long time, and second-guessing myself in the best way.

Maybe I could have it all.

Then Sunday morning rolled around, and I checked my email to find that word had gotten around about my business.

"How much to ship to Toronto?"

"Can you have one ready by Friday?"

And then there were the orders. My seventeen orders were now thirty-two. This was a problem I never saw coming. No one thinks their business is going to do too well.

Fuck.

Before I could panic too hard, Ben came down the stairs. "Hey Mom, I need to get my tux for prom, and order a corsage for my date."

"Morning to you, too."

He put some bread into the toaster. "Morning! Oh, and my tuition deposit is due at the college, and I can't figure out how to pay it online. They have a weird transfer system that makes no sense. Can you have a look? The deposit is due tomorrow."

"Yeah, no problem." The words didn't match the swirling in my gut. I had to get these nightstands done; I had to answer the emails, I had shifts this week at the diner, and of course my son came first.

I took a deep breath and did what moms do. I shoved my overwhelm aside and got shit done. "Make an appointment to get fitted for a tux. Try for Tuesday because I don't work at the diner, so you can take my car. Find out what color your date's dress is, then we can order a corsage to match. Call the college, and use my credit card to pay the deposit."

"Thanks, Mom," he said around a bite of toast.

I snatched a piece of paper from my notebook and started making a to-do list. I needed groceries, to put money on my credit card for the tuition, to make sure I booked the day of the prom off so I could see my only son go off to the big dance. I needed more supplies to do the nightstands. The list kept going, and nowhere on it was there a sweet man with hair that fell in his eyes and a smile that brought one to my face.

I ran a hand through my hair and headed to the garage. I didn't have time to dwell on that right now; I had shit to do.

I spent every waking minute that I wasn't busy with work or Ben in the garage or doing supply runs to Springwood.

Chapter Seventeen

Wyatt texted me a few times, and I felt awful about how long it took me to get back to him. All I sent him was a few words in reply. I didn't want to give him up, I really didn't, but I didn't see how I could keep him either. He deserved someone as thoughtful and giving as he was, and I just didn't know how to be that person and still keep my life going.

Every time I finished an order, more had come in, and my to-do list kept growing.

I had to research shipping costs. I was looking into whether I could send them out unassembled with the hardware and instructions.

People were asking about different colors of stains or custom paint jobs, hardware options. This was so much bigger than I was ready for, and I couldn't think about the big picture when I had a stack of order confirmations in front of me that needed to be filled.

Thursday after dinner my phone rang, and Wyatt's name flashed across the screen. I hesitated before picking it up. In my mind, if I didn't say the words and tell him I couldn't do this with him, then it wasn't true, but I couldn't avoid this forever.

"Hi," I said.

"Hey, you seemed too busy to text this week, so I wanted to call."

I ran a hand through my hair and realized I needed to wash it. "Yeah, I got a flood of orders for more night stands, I barely have time to eat or sleep, and Ben has some stuff to do for graduation and..."

"And you don't have time for another thing in your life right now."

It wasn't a question, but I answered anyway. "Yeah, that is about what it comes down to."

I chewed the side of my lip, not sure if I should take back everything I said and go see him, or crawl into a corner and cry.

I wanted it all. I wanted my cake and to eat it too. The fact that I couldn't had never been an issue before, but now, faced with losing Wyatt, I wanted to throw a tantrum like a toddler about how unfair it all was.

"I'm sorry."

"Look, Vera, I understand you have a lot going on, and it sounds like things are chaotic for you right now. I won't reach out if you don't want me to. I don't want you to feel like I'm something on your to-do list that you have to stress about getting to."

God, it sounded so awful when he put it that way.

"Can you do me one little favor?"

I blew out a breath. "What is it?"

"Just don't give up on us yet, okay?"

My heart did a stupid little skip, and I found myself nodding. "Okay, I promise I won't."

"Thanks, Vera. Get some sleep, okay? Things have a way of working out."

Don't give up.

That was easier said than done.

I woke up on Friday morning to the sound of someone knocking on my front door. I hadn't slept nearly as much as I should have, but the knocking didn't stop.

I shuffled to the front door in a t-shirt and shorts, hair in something that resembled a messy bun and a hurricane in one. I opened the door and Wyatt was standing there, looking unfairly good in jeans, a flannel shirt with a tool belt around his waist. It was a flashback to the first time he stood on my doorstep, except now I knew how good it felt to have his arms around me, and how much it hurt not to have them there again.

"Morning," he handed me a to-go cup and a bag with the Bend's Best Brew logo on the side. I took them dumbly, still half asleep. "What's going on?"

Another Wild Timber truck pulled into my driveway, and two men I vaguely recognized got out.

Wyatt beamed. "We're having a slow day at Wild Timber today; materials delay, again. So Zane, Elias, and I are going to help you build nightstands."

"But...you don't have to do that." Rejecting help was my default setting, and I jumped to it even though I desperately needed the help.

He rested a hand on each of my arms, and the simple touch had my shoulders relaxing. "I know we don't, and I know you don't like to accept help. You would figure this all out without me, but sometimes if a hand is offered, you should just take it. I also know that if I'm going to convince you to go out on a second date, I have to show you that I'm all in. Not just for dinners out and sex, but for the day-to-day stuff too. Stuff with Ben or work or your business. You know?"

My heart started to melt and my sleep-deprived eyes watered.

"I want to kiss you and have fun with you, but I also want to be there when you're stressed or get you coffee when you've had a hard day."

"Wyatt, I—I'm a mess." I gestured with my hand, which was holding the coffee, to my worn-out clothes.

"And I'm here to help clean it up. And one day, when I'm a mess, you'll clean me up too. That's what you want, right? A partner, not another obligation."

"This is a lot of sweet things to say first thing in the morning. But yeah, that's what I want."

"Daylight's wasting," Elias called from behind us.

"Go have breakfast, okay? Drink some coffee, then meet us in the garage, and we'll get as many of these things built as we can."

I was tired, hungry, undercaffeinated, in desperate need of a shower, and completely overwhelmed. But I was also determined to make this business work, and Wyatt was offering me a lifeline.

I stepped back to let the guys in, then grabbed the breakfast sandwich from the bag and shoved it in my mouth as I ran up the stairs to get dressed. I didn't have time to dawdle over coffee; I had three trained carpenters here offering to help, and I needed to take advantage.

The things that Wyatt had said circled in my mind as I pulled on some jeans, but I didn't have time to dwell on them now. I had pushed him away because I couldn't see how everything could work.

He was here to show me how wrong I was. I wanted to be wrong.

I just wasn't in any position to decide right now. I needed to clear my head, and to do that I needed to clear the backlog of nightstands.

We set up an assembly line in the garage. I organized while Elias did the initial cuts, Zane did the assembly, and Wyatt sanded and stained.

The guys worked hard. We got a sizable amount of my orders done, or partly done by the time five o'clock rolled around and Zane and Elias said goodbye.

Wyatt was putting the finishing touches on one of the nightstands as I finally had time to look around and see what we had accomplished.

Wyatt had shown up for me in a way I wasn't sure anyone ever had, and my heart was singing his praises. "Do you have to go, too?" I asked.

He stood up and crossed the garage to stand in front of me. "Do you want me to?"

I shook my head. "I want you to stay."

Chapter Eighteen

Wyatt

It had been a busy day.

Physically, I was tired from the work, but when Vera took my hand and led me to her shower, the exhaustion evaporated. "Do you want to talk about everything you said when you got here?"

I turned the shower on to let it warm up and moved to face her. She looked completely worn out. The fact that she wanted me here was good enough for now. We could sort the rest out later. "We can talk about it later. For now can we just say that we want to make this work?"

"I do want that, so much. How about we shower, order pizza and eat it in my bed?"

"That sounds like heaven."

She leaned in and kissed me, soft and slow. She smelled like sawdust, tasted like sweat and her. She took the hem of my shirt in her hands and pulled it up, breaking the kiss to get it over my head. A puff of dust filled the air as she pulled it away.

Our lips met as we stripped each other, not demanding or escalating, just contact after a long week.

Once we were down to nothing, we stepped under the warm spray of the shower together. She wrapped her arms around me and rested her head against my chest. "I'm sorry I didn't answer your texts all week. I didn't want to let you go, but I didn't know how we could make this work."

I kissed the top of her head. "I was afraid of the same thing. I'm glad I called."

"I'm glad I answered and that you're here now."

"Me too, so long as we both want this, we will find a way to make it happen."

She looked up and met my eyes. "Promise?"

"Promise." We brought our lips together, again. The teasing from last time was gone. I wasn't trying to prove anything or desperate to scratch an itch. This was just her and me, stripped bare, taking comfort and pleasure where we could get it in life.

She dragged her fingertips over the ridges of my chest and down until she grasped my hard cock and gently stroked it bringing it fully to life.

I pulled my lips from hers, letting my head fall back just enjoying the feel of her hands on my skin.

I moved my hand between us, sliding it between her folds until I found her clit then circled it with my calloused finger tip. She brought her free hand to my shoulder, clinging to me, her fingers leaving marks on my skin. We stayed like that, water cascading over our naked bodies, sharing the same air.

She was letting out short little breaths as I worked her over and precum oozed from my tip. I was getting close already, but I didn't want to finish in her hand. I wanted to be buried inside her, connected in the most intimate way.

I grabbed one of her thighs, bringing it up over my hip.

I felt the heat of her center against my skin, smelled her shampoo in the confined space.

I took my cock in my hand, hard as steel from her skilled touch, and brought it to her entrance. Her wet heat against the head of my cock had fire licking through my veins. My legs and back were sore from the day's work, but the pain melted away. I hunched a little to get the angle right before sliding into her, her body exciting and familiar at the same time.

Her warmth hugged every inch of me, and I moved my hips, slow at first but getting faster. I was driven by pure instinct and need. Chasing a high that only she could provide.

"You feel so good, Wyatt," she said. I loved the sound of my name from her lips when her voice was strained.

We stared into each other's eyes as I moved, pleasure bursting through me every time I sank in deep.

"I'm close," she said, leaning in and taking my lips with hers. I kissed her back, tasting her before sliding my tongue into her mouth. The kiss grew more frantic until her breath caught and she came apart in my arms. I followed right after, pumping her full of my cum, holding her body as it sagged against me and her knees went weak.

After a week of not knowing if I could ever have her again, I was satisfied in more ways than one when we shut the water off.

Once we'd dried off, we settled into her bed with a pizza. Her in an oversized t-shirt, me naked since my clothes from the day were filthy.

The whole room smelled like her, and we sank into the mattress shoulder to shoulder while we made quick work of the food.

"You're staying the night, right?" She asked, tucking her wet hair behind her ear.

"I want to, but is it okay that I'm here? Ben will see my truck out front."

Vera looked up at me, impossibly beautiful even when she was tired and had worked hard all day. "You're going to be around a lot, so I'll have to tell him about us. Just a few days of thinking I couldn't have you was bad enough, now I never want to let you go."

Epilogue - Six Months Later

Vera

Today was moving day. In more ways than one. Not only was Ben moving into the dorms in Springwood, but I was moving in with Wyatt.

I had sold my house. The new owners took possession in a month, so I had some time to get the whole place cleaned out. Still, this day was going to be a long one.

It was stressful, but not overwhelming. Not when I had Wyatt and the loyal group of people from Wild Timber Homes who were always willing to lend a hand.

I looked around me at the house where I'd raised my son, where I'd struggled and persevered, where I'd decided to try again when it came to love. There were so many good memories here, but I was ready to move on. Wyatt had set up half of his garage as a workspace for me to build the nightstands so I was there a lot during the day anyway, and we hadn't spent a night apart since we told Ben about us.

Epilogue - Six Months Later

Wyatt came into the room wearing work boots, jeans, and a white t-shirt that would be dirt-colored by the end of the day. He pulled me into a hug, and I melted against his chest. "Are you ready for this?"

"The hard work, leaving my house behind, or my son going off to college?"

He laughed, "All three, I guess."

I blew out a breath. "No, yes, and sort of." The front door opened and my ex, Scott, came through it. He had arranged his schedule so that he could see Ben off to college, too. Wyatt stuck out his hand, and the two men shook.

"Ready to drop our kid off at college?" he asked me.

"Ready or not, today's the day."

"Jace, Elias, and Zane are going to help me start moving your stuff to my place while you guys are moving Ben's stuff. Does that work?"

"I feel bad leaving you to deal with all this."

He laughed and kissed my temple. "I don't mind. I know Ben says he's all grown up, but he'll want you there, both of you."

"He's right," Scott said. "We never could help him with his math homework; at least we can move some boxes."

I laughed. "Alright, let's get this kid's stuff loaded up."

Ben, Scott and I each took our own cars, filled with stuff to Springwood. Ben was staying. Scott was headed to work afterwards, and I was headed to Wyatt's, so we each needed our own vehicles. It was weirdly symbolic of us each going our own way.

Damn it, now I was fighting back tears.

When we pulled up to the dorm building, the parking lot was packed, and there were people everywhere. We managed to find spots and grabbed a cart.

It was a disorganized disaster, but we got him all moved in.

"Well, I guess that's it," Ben said, looking around the cramped space. They were single-occupancy rooms, about eight by ten feet, with a bed, desk, fridge, and a small counter with a hot plate. Four rooms connected together into one common area with a bathroom.

"Proud of you, son," Scott said, pulling him against his chest and hugging him tight. Ben was tall like his dad, but still on the skinny side. He looked very much like a kid next to his barrel-chested dad.

Ben pulled away and came to me, letting me hug him tight. "I'm going to miss you. You call if you need anything, okay? Anything." I'd been reminding myself to call him Ben, not Benji, after Wyatt mentioned it.

"I know, Mom, and thanks."

"You don't have to thank me; this is what parents are for."

"I know, but still, thanks."

We had come to a compromise a week before. Ben would pay for his living expenses, but Scott and I were splitting the cost of his tuition. It was a compromise none of us were happy with, so that is how we knew it was right. Ben wanted to pay all of it, and so did we.

One of the other kids in his dorm arrived, and Ben waved to us so he could go introduce himself.

"We raised a good kid," Scott said as we walked to the parking lot.

"We did. You off for another long haul trip?"

He sighed. "Yeah," he sounded tired, and I reminded myself it wasn't my place to suggest he find a career that let him sleep and see his kid more.

"You off to Wyatt's place?"

I nodded.

"I like him. I'm happy for you guys."

"Thanks, you'll find someone one of these days too, assuming that's what you want."

"We'll see." He was as resigned to his fate as I had been before I met Wyatt.

I made the drive back to Wildrose Bend, filled my SUV at my old house, then headed to Wyatt's house. Our house now.

I pulled into the driveway around dinnertime. It had taken longer than I'd expected to move things at Ben's dorm, and now my energy for moving things was flagging.

Wyatt bounded down the steps and met me at my car door with a kiss. "How did it go?"

"Good, took a while, but he seems happy."

He nodded. "Let's get your SUV unloaded, then get some dinner."

We did exactly that, and by the time the sun started to dip. We were cuddled together on his couch with boxes and suitcases strewn around the room. "Thanks for doing all the moving today," I said, head resting on his shoulder, eyes closed as the TV droned quietly in the background.

He kissed my temple. "You don't have to thank me. Partners, right?"

I nodded, breathing in his scent. "I love you Wyatt."

"Love you too, Vera."

I tightened my arms around him.

After my divorce, even though it was civil as far as divorces went, I'd fought for everything. I'd worked, and I'd scraped and saved and compromised and given more than I took.

Finally, I'd found some semblance of peace, and I'd risked it all. I'd gambled on the goofy carpenter with the too-long hair and the sweet smile, and I'd won.

I'd won a peace that was deeper and richer than I ever thought I'd have again.

Enjoying your stay in Wildrose Bend? Find out if Zane finds love in Wood you be Mine, available on Amazon May 3rd!

Did you miss Layne and Elias's story? Check out Lumber and Lace on Amazon!

Eager for more Lumberjacks? Brody, owner of Two Rivers Tree Falling has his own romance in Felled by the Lumberjack, available on Amazon April 19th

Check out my full catalog!

Highway of Love Series

Tow the Line
A Wrench in the Plan
For the Long Haul
Go the Extra Mile
Going the Distance
The Wheels Fall Off

Strawberry Hill Search and Rescue Series

A Rescue for the Mountain Man
A Detour for the Mountain Man
A New Start for the Mountain Man

Vegas Vows

Beauty and the Builder
Grease and Glamour
Pretty in Paint

Wild Timber Homes

Lumber and Lace
Rough Cut Romance
Wood you be Mine

Sage Valley Standalones

Mr. Write
Just Screwing Around
Making a Mountain Man

Christmas

Snowed in with the Blue-Collar Billionaire
Teaching Christmas to the Mountain Man

Multi-Author Series

Her Protective Biker
Unplanned Mountain Man
Butting Heads with the Bodyguard
Felled by the Lumberjack

About the Author

Alana Gray is a Canadian writer hoping to prove that romance doesn't end when you turn thirty.

She lives in the interior of British Columbia with her husband, daughter, and one sassy cat. These beautiful surroundings inspire blue-collar characters, unpredictable weather, and forced proximity sparks to fly.

Visit www.AuthorAlanaGray.com to see my full list of books!

www.ingramcontent.com/pod-product-compliance
Lightning Source LLC
LaVergne TN
LVHW051013080826
845145LV00009B/2604

* 9 7 8 1 0 6 7 5 3 5 8 0 3 *